MILLER HOMES II

FIVE YEARS LATER

CHARLES FEGGANS

Copyright © 2023 Charles Feggans.

All rights reserved. No part of this book may be reproduced, stored, or transmitted by any means—whether auditory, graphic, mechanical, or electronic—without written permission of both publisher and author, except in the case of brief excerpts used in critical articles and reviews. Unauthorized reproduction of any part of this work is illegal and is punishable by law.

ISBN: 979-8-89031-815-2 (sc)
ISBN: 979-8-89031-816-9 (hc)
ISBN: 979-8-89031-817-6 (e)

Because of the dynamic nature of the Internet, any web addresses or links contained in this book may have changed since publication and may no longer be valid. The views expressed in this work are solely those of the author and do not necessarily reflect the views of the publisher, and the publisher hereby disclaims any responsibility for them.

One Galleria Blvd., Suite 1900, Metairie, LA 70001
(504) 702-6708

CHAPTER One

It has been a little more than five years since Bertha left Tower One structure at Miller Homes. During her absence, the unsightly building and area had deteriorated even more, leaving a rundown grayish color building that blended in with the dry concrete pavement and surrounding other structures leaving them almost hollow from lack of maintenance showing broken glass windows covered with boards and a variety of colorful graffiti where tenants use to reside.

The parking area located to the side of the buildings, featured vehicles with flat tires, broken wind shields and some faded paintings designs by small piles of unsightly liter. Low lining surrounded trees with many broken branches used by children for recreation covered several parts of parked vehicles. Beside them is an empty playground with a dirty sandbox, a rusty slide, a partly rusty bench with one missing board and a swing set with only one functional seat and two hanging chains with no attacked seats. Near the front of both Towers, a warn pick nick bench set continues to provide seating in fairly good condition. The original color has long been washed away by the changing seasons of hot, cold, rain and snowy weather conditions.

On this very day, a light breeze shifts through the parking lot blowing around trash and dry leaves, causing liter to pile up in parts of the area. Pigeons moving around on the ground began flying away after pecking and feeding on food containers containing particles of food scraps.

With all the efforts and available resources at hand, a new mayor failed to gain support from tenants to keep Miller Homes a pride of the city. Some tenants had no respect for keeping the area clean. Most felt that as rent paying tenants, it was the city's job to maintain a safe and clean environment. So trashy items continued to flourish throughout the area.

Miller Homes was located in a low income area where most people living in the middle and upper class housing area tried to avoid areas like Miller Homes. This is mostly where drug dealers and gangs seemed to hangout. Law enforcement found it almost impossible to rid Miller Homes of the drug dealers and gangs who sold their drugs and created problems for tenants and visitors. Many of these criminal out case lived in the towers where residents loved feeding on them. Outsiders and residents who purchased products from dealers refused to give up names to the proper authorities that would identify dealers and gang members for fear of repercussions.

Gangs continued to roam through the area creating problem and terrorizing residents to a point where as night fell, most residents chose not to leave their apartment in fear of being harassed, assaulted or possibly killed. And so, the night and part of the day light hours belong to the trouble makers and drug dealers who controlled Miller Homes.

It was a bright sunny day as a group of happy teenagers came walking toward the parking area. They laughed and pushed at each other in a joking manner. The group suddenly decided to separate and go their separate ways, leaving a single teenager in his tracks. The teenager shouted to the group, "A' ight, see ya." And he goes on his merry way in a different direction away from the group.

Bertha returned to Miller Homes with Breeze because life in the country wasn't what she had expected it to be. Living far from the next farm, no excitement around the farm and seeing very few visitors. She felt lost most of the time. Other than that, she and Breeze helped around the farm as much as possible. That was just about the only work they could find. Bertha though by her and Breeze helping with the farm needs, this would compensate for not paying rent and board.

The only enjoyment Bertha could get out of life was going to church. This was a Sunday thing where she was able to meet with others and share in having a good time. But that only lasted for that day. Church did things with its people such as having programs, gatherings and events, going places and having classes on bible verses and matters of every day concerns. This mostly consisted of being with church folks for a full day. Breeze loved that day and couldn't wait for the next Sunday to come. He had made friends with many of the teenagers around his age and they enjoyed each other.

It may have been a GOD's blessing that sent Bertha and her family to the country. There she learned that GOD was a real spirit and had a name which many people called JEHOVAH. And his son Jesus Christ name is Michael. GOD sent Bertha help through her girlfriend Monique to let her see she needed help. Things started off bad back in Trenton's Miller Homes with guys chasing after her and her daughter, who were up to no good and doing no good deeds. Her boyfriend Butch, who hung around Miller Homes as a loner, lost her stereo set in a parking lot fight and ended up getting himself badly hurt. Later, he was murdered on the streets by a gang leader who went by the name of Flash. Then, she found out that her son Breeze was tied in with a king pin named Sonny Bee, who had him selling drugs to make himself wealthy.

For the many times Bertha went to see the mayor about cleaning up Miller Homes, all he and the police chief did was give out promises that was never fulfilled. She tried working with some of the residents, but they felt it was too dangerous out and about with the drug dealers and a gang acting up at times. After becoming totally depressed with this situation and not having a job to go to plus living on government assistance, she fell into a slump and allowed herself to become friendly with a drug dealer who did nothing but bring her down to her lowest point in life. Breeze tried to break his mother away from the scene by stop funding her with money, but the drug dealer she connected with loved her so much that he provided her with most of the drugs she asked for even after their money had dried up. It took her girlfriend, Monique with a lot of force and persuasion to get her to understand that this was no life for her. So, Bertha agreed under pressure to enter a drug rehabilitation program. Upon completion, she was able to learn a skill that would help her to support herself and family once she got herself straightened out. Realizing it was time for her to move on with her life. She gathered up her two kids and headed south.

After living in the country for the first several months with no real job and very few friends, Bertha began to realize living in Miller Homes wasn't as bad as she and some people claimed it to be. People were friendly and they were everywhere. Not like in the country. Maybe the problem was that those who never lived in government housing didn't understand the life Miller Homes people had to endure. Renaming 'Miller Homes' as 'Killer Homes,' Bertha thought was going a little too far. Maybe the mayor changed the name because during her five year absent, 19 people had been murdered and another 45 had been assaulted. Some had to be hospitalized because of injuries. However, like most developments, Miller Homes was having its problems as well such as gangs, people breaking into apartments, rundown conditions that was slowly or never repaired and unwanted visitors just hanging around.

In Miller Homes, there was something here for her. Places she could walk to and be active in the community. Or sit around day after day when she wasn't doing things around the apartment or amusing herself thinking about the good and not so good times she spent with her son Breeze and an occasional visit from her daughter Mary.

Bertha was glad about a few things like moving away from Miller Homes when she did. No telling what might have happened to her trying to rid Miller Homes from those drug dealers and gangs. Plus giving the mayor a hard time in trying to clean up Miller Homes. And poor Breeze, who was just 14 years old at the time, might have been caught up in some kind of mess that might have ended up with him dead or getting a police record for life. Happily, while he was in the south, he returned to school and graduated from High School. He was also taking cooking classes during his last 2 years. This made her feel proud that he would be able to cook for both himself and his mom during times when she was too tired to cook herself. He was now living at home with Bertha and working a real job. "Amen," she would always say to that.

As for Mary, her daughter had also graduated from High School with honors and was now freely living in the country away from guys who called themselves thugs and was always pressuring her because she was an attractive female and smart. Bertha also felt proud that Mary had turned out to be a very good daughter with a good head on her shoulders. She did the best thing by staying in the south with her aunt.

Now that Bertha was back living in Miller Homes, she had connected with a few of her old friends and made some new ones as well. One of her new friends was Sally. She was someone Bertha could sit and discuss her personal business and problems with. Sally was an overly middle age single woman who never married. Had plenty of men friends but never had any children. She was one of the first residents to have moved into Miller Homes when they were new. Sally was a home body who loved staying in her apartment. At present, she didn't work due to an injury she received from a job she had worked on many, many years ago. Although she didn't work, she always had plenty of things to do.

On a particular morning, Sally was sitting in her favorite recliner located in a dark corner of her living room watching her favorite morning program. While enjoying the action taking place before her on the screen, she became overly excited and accidently spilled hot liquid from a cup she was holding onto her night gown. The heated liquid caused her to squirm wildly in her seat. The expression on her face quickly changed instantly from the sudden surprise of joy from the program to a sudden sadness as she viewed the heated stained mess created before her. Being she could not reverse the damage, she sat the remaining content in the cup on an end table and started walking toward the kitchen while hand brushing at the creeping, stained, liquid that seemed to slowly motion its way toward the edge of her garment. "I'll have to throw this garment away. What a mess." Suddenly the doorbell began to ring. Sally stopped in her tracks thinking. *'Who could that be this early in the morning?'* The bell rang again. Changing her stepping direction, she headed toward the door. Upon opening it, she found herself face to face with Bertha who she hadn't seen in what she called a month of Sundays.

Bertha had met Sally one day while she was out sitting on the bench in the courtyard of Miller Homes. They started a conversation and that lead to a binding friendship. With a look of surprise on Sally's face, she was glad to extend a warm greeting toward her. "What a surprise," said Sally. "Don't just stand there. Come on in."

"Since you put it that way, how can I refuse," replied Bertha with a smile. Sally, still feeling the wetness of liquid on her clothing, looked down and was quick to make a remark that things happen and this was one of her bad mornings. She hoped the rest of the day would get better.

While entering the apartment, Bertha was quick to make comment. "Girl, you're gonna be fine. I get those days sometimes myself. I call them acts of mishaps."

"You better believe it," replied Sally.

As bertha walked into the front room, she couldn't help but to notice a wide arrangement of different items placed around the room. The one outstanding thing that quickly caught her attention was a very young picture of Sally mounted over the fireplace. Casually she walked over to look at it. Looking straight into the picture, she smiled. "Sally." She called out. "This is really a nice picture of you when you was just a little girl."

Sally was quick to respond. "Really? We getting up in age and I don't feel the same now as I did back then. Pains are starting to set in all over my body."

"I know what you mean. My friend Mark is a pain in the you know what."

"Oh. I can deal with that kind of pain. But those other pains. Girl, you just don't know. Have a seat. I wanna hear what's going on in your life, If I can ask?" Sally went to turn off the television and made herself comfortable in a seat next to Bertha. "After watching so much Television, I can't believe what's happening in this world of ours these days," Sally said. "This world is really, and I do mean really whacky. I can't imagine what's going to happen next. All I know is that people are killing each other like crazy and robbing each other over what seems to be a misunderstanding, greed or something crazy. It's really terrible I tell you."

"No. I mean how new things are just pushing old things off to one side. I can remember as far back as when I was around 5 years old."

Sally started laughing. "You must have a good memory. Girl, I can't remember the days of the week or what I ate for breakfast yesterday." They both joined in on a laugh.

"Neither can I sometimes. As I was saying, I remember seeing a horse drawn carriage coming around my street and this old man was selling things. And the one horse drawn carriage would leave deposits on the street that really smelt bad. Now we have cars racing up and down the streets polluting the air. What a change."

Sally acted as though she was working her thinking cap. "Interesting. Yeah. That was long ago. You're right. Our minds seem to let things like that go."

Bertha started placing her hands over her stomach. A sharp pain was causing her to slightly bend at the waist.

Sally saw what was happening and became worried. "Bertha! What's going on?"

Bertha could hardly speak. "It's my stomach. I have been having these instant pains off and on for the past several months."

"You need to see a Doctor."

"I know. But for the time being, it's okay. It only last for a minute or two."

"It could be serious. You really do need to see one as soon as possible."

"I'm taking something for it." Bertha reached into her pocket book and takes out a small bottle of pills. She downed two and asked for a glass of water. Sally goes into kitchen and returned. Bertha drinks it in two sips. Sally received the glass and places it on the floor near her feet.

"I'm starting to feel better."

"Girl. That stuff must really act fast. I hope you know what you're doing."

"The man at the drug store said these pill would kill the pain." Bertha straightened up to lean back onto her seat. "Let me tell you. It's funny how these memories come back to us. And the funny thing about living in the city with neighborhoods like mine, people didn't have locks on their doors in those days. The funny thing about this is that I never heard of anyone ever being robbed. And in today's time, I tell you, people will break into your home if it is locked or not. And the sad part of it is, they don't care if you're at home or away. Did you know back in the early 1950's, a lot of homes still had outhouses in the city?"

"That I do remember. I can still feel chills thinking about it. Sitting on that stool was like sitting on a block of ice in the winter."

They both laughed.

Bertha was acting as though she was feeling chills. "Our home was one of them. I remember having to go to the outhouse in the winter when it was freezing cold and even in the snow. It was just like being outside without any clothes."

"But you did have a bathroom, didn't you?"

"No. Believe it or not. As far as I can remember, my mother use to give me a bath in the kitchen, in a large galvanize round tub that sat in the middle of the floor. I don't know how the rest of the family washed themselves. Some years later after we moved away from that street, bathrooms were already built into newer homes. I was glad we moved into one. It was small with a tub, sink and toilet."

Sally smiled as if wanting to say something but held it to herself. She did open up to say, "There's no way I could imagine having a home without a bathroom in these days. We were blessed enough to have one inside."

"You must remember that, that was then, and things are different now. We living in a whole new world."

"I know girl. Let me tell you. This world is moving so fast, I'm losing sight of where I stand. This computer age has gotten my mine so twisted with ordering stuff online that I'm always ordering the wrong size or they're sending to me the wrong item."

"I know just what you mean. The old days were the best. We didn't have these problems. You just reminded me of the time my mom and one of her sisters would take me to the grocery store. The first thing they would do when entering the store was to grab a bag of grapes and they would eat every grape by the end of our shopping trip."

"Didn't they worry about getting caught for stealing?"

"No. They were just doing what they saw lots of other people doing. Even today I still see people doing that."

"Girl. You had a lot going on in your earlier years."

"I guess we all have a lot in our memory bank. We just won't let things out."

"I guess you're right. One of my aunt's boyfriends who use to come to our home often was told by my mom to shape up my hair. She would always say my hair looked like the rats been sucking on it with the ends all out of shape being long in some areas and short in others."

Sally couldn't help but to break out into a string of laughter. "Rats sucking on your hair. What more could they do or say about you?"

"While he was trying to cut my hair, he made a statement that the hand clippers he was using wasn't sharp enough to cut my wire like hair. My mom got mad at him for making that statement, so he placed the clippers over top of my grandmother's China cabinet. Well, little old me didn't believe him. I think he just didn't want to be fooling around with my hair. So, while everyone was not around, I climbed to the top of the cabinet. Just as I reached the top, and had my hands on the clippers, the cabinet fell over, breaking up much of the China ware. I was just trying to prove that my aunt's boyfriend he was wrong by me cutting off some of my own hair."

"So, what happened?"

"My mom came down after hearing the crash. She cleaned up everything. She did say if it happens again, she would beat the living day light out of me."

"Look like you got away with murder that time."

"Yeah." Bertha had to stop and think for a moment. She had gotten carried away with talking about her own personal life. Maybe she shouldn't have given all these secrets away. However, it felt good for once getting some of these old memories off her chest. All her friends knew how she loved to talk. And Sally was a good listener. Being she was on a roll. She couldn't stop.

"Check this out." Bertha started showing signs of getting excited She went on to say. "When I was around five years old, I was allowed to play with some of the neighborhood kids. This one day, my grandmother let some of the neighborhood kids come inside our home and we all went to play in the basement. We did this for as long as I can remember. Well, my grandfather slept in the basement. Why. I will never get the true meaning. He had all these clothes and ties hanging everywhere. The hanging ties made the basement look like a picture from a Tarzan Jungle movie." Sally laughed. "Anyway, someone came up with the idea that we could use matches to light candles that was laying around. So, we lit them, turned out the lights and played around in the semi-dark. It was fun. However, I don't remember how it happened or who did it, but somebody knocked over one of the candles, setting some of the clothes on fire."

Sally said. "Oh no," while placing her hand against her mouth.

"Not knowing what to do, all of us ran up the steps. The smell from the fire followed us. My grandmother, who was in the kitchen at the time, caught wind of the smoke and called the fire department. Luckily the fire department wasn't too far away. They arrived in time to reduce any major damage. And also, the door to the basement was in the kitchen so, it didn't take much for my grandmother to catch wind of the smoke. That was the last time any of the kids from the neighborhood was allowed in our home."

Sally started to laugh through her mumbling. "You little fire bug. What did you grandmother say to you?"

"Never again was I to have kids come inside this house."

"That must have been some ordeal."

"I can never forget it. It was scary. We didn't know how to put the fire out. That's why we ran up the step. So, one of the neighbors across the street bought a television. The first one in our neighborhood. Mine you. This was back in the late 1940's. My mom took me to that house and left me with the owner. A lot of other kids were there also. I remember seeing the screen being round and sizable so you could sit just about anywhere in the front room and still see the picture. The screen in those days had a thin plastic sheet across the face with three sections of colors. Top one-third had a thin yellow plastic covering. The middle was red, and the bottom was blue. This was called color television."

"It must have been funny to look at."

"I don't recall. I was just a little kid in the bunch. I was just amazed to see something like that. By the time we got a television, they were being made in Black and White. It was the changing of times. Today, we have televisions that can do just about anything. Better known as SMART TELEVISIONS."

"I don't think I could live in a home without a television." Sally jumped in to say.

"Before then, we listened to radio. There were some great stories and music on it. Like The Shadow, Lone Ranger, Amos and Andy, Jack Benny and others. I really didn't care too much for the glass 78 records. My aunts played enough of that mess to turn me off. But Somehow, I miss though days."

"You have had such an exciting early life."

"It's funny how we can remember that far back." Bertha looked at her watch. "Oh. I need to be going. You know how some people are when it comes to being not on time for work."

"I know what you mean. Been there myself," said Sally. "We need to get together more often. You are such good company. I'm glad you stopped bye."

"Next time I won't talk your head off."

Sally reached out and touched Bertha's hand. "Oh, I don't mind. I love to hear you talk about the old days. They have me thinking about some of my mishaps and good times."

"I'm glad to see that." Bertha glanced down at her watch again. "Well, I'll be going." Bertha stood and walked toward the door. Sally followed. Bertha exited and with a wave of her hand, said, "Take care."

Sally stood for a moment to watch Bertha as she swayed a little in walking away. Suddenly, Sally called out, "Take care of that stomach problem."

Bertha replied without looking back. "I will. I got this."

Sally said to herself. "Amazing woman." And returned to her apartment.

CHAPTER Two

After weeks of searching for a job, Bertha had previously found a job before her last visit to see Sally. It was an office job for which she had trained as a Clerk Typist. At first, she found the job to be interesting, but as weeks passed she soon became bored with the position and lost interest. It was the type of job where she sat all day with no outlet. Soon she felt she was wasting her God given talent on a job that seemed to be going nowhere. She wanted something that was a more livelier job with an opportunity to do something she liked and possibly help her develop newer skills.

One evening while walking home, she spotted a sign in a local beauty salon window asking for help. She walked up close to the salon and looked through the window of this small run-down salon with worn out chairs and slightly discolored mirrors. The salon seemed almost empty except for one worker working on a customer and another sitting on a side chair waiting her turn to have her needs taken care of. Bertha walked away thinking this might be something she would like to do. After all, she was doing her own hair and nails. Why not do other people's hair and nails. It probably paid more with salary and tips that she was presently making from her present job.

That night she thought more and more about the job. The next day after work, she went in to talk with the owner. After having a short conversation, she felt this was the job for her, so she applied. During their conversation she felt she had to explain that she didn't have to much experience working on other people's heads and nails, but was a quick learner and had been doing her own hair and nails for many years. Because the owner was in very much need of help, she was willing to accept her on a trial bases.

A week later, Bertha changed jobs and went in to work at the salon. She found the work easy, enjoyable and the other workers very friendly. From them, she learned different styles and ways to make her work easier from those who were willing to teach her.

It was a late night and the salon had just closed. Bertha was sweeping hair into a dust bin and placing several tools into a basket near a styling chair. She turned to her co-worker, who was the salon owner. "Are you closing up shop this evening?"

Her co-worker continuing to set things in place. She replied without looking toward Bertha. "Yeah. Why? You got somewhere to be?"

"No. Not really." Bertha replied. "Just got'ta get home to feed my kid. You know how they love to eat." She began to laugh nervously. Not wanting to let her know Breeze was a 19 year old teenager on his way to becoming a man. Her co-worker stopped to look at the clock. The time on the wall indicated it was 8 p.m. In a tired voice she says to Bertha, "Look at that. We really had a busy day. Girl I feel really worn out."

Bertha wiped her hands with a washcloth and takes out her jumper from a bag she carriers every day to work. "Alright girl. Done cleaning. All you need to do is close shop. See you tomorrow." She looks at herself in the mirror while letting her hair down. Strands of lose hairs had fallen across her face. She neatly placed them on her head and began putting on her jumper that was unzipped and grabbed her bag. Her co-worker sees Bertha walking toward the door. She called out. "Be safe out there. This is a bad neighborhood. Full of crime and who knows what else is going on this time of night."

Bertha smiled and replied, "Yeah. I know. I don't live too far from here. Bye." And she passes through the door and out onto the sidewalk.

As she walks along, a light breeze began to blow her hair around. A few men hanging around across the street began whistling at her as she passes them. One calls out. "Hey beautiful." The other men laughed. She starts walking a little faster, ignoring them and began to show signs of becoming uncomfortable. She zips up her jumper close to her neck and clutches her bag closer to her chest.

Several fast cars zoom pass her at high speed causing her hair to move wildly around her head. The men across the street continue laughing in a distance. Bertha now nervous, looks at the ground so she would be careful not to make eye contact with other pedestrians as she pass by them.

Finally, Bertha arrived at Miller Homes. As she enters the lobby, she sees Flash's Aunt struggling to carry several grocery packages as she makes her way toward the elevator. Bertha sees the sign above the elevator in big black letters. 'ELEVATOR OUT OF ORDER.' "Auntie," she calls out as she quickly approaches her. "We can't use these elevators. They ain't working."

Auntie looks up to see Bertha. "My Dear. What was I thinking! I keep forgetting these things don't work. I guess I'm showing my memory is going bad."

"Don't say that Auntie. Let me help you with these packages." Bertha says politely, "We need to walk up the steps. I don't know if they are ever going to fix these elevators. They haven't worked in months."

"It's a shame they aren't thinking about us older folks and some of the handy cap people. I'm glad you asked. Thank you dear. Take this bag. These steps are going to be the death of me someday." Auntie hands Bertha a sagging bag she is trying to hold onto.

"Tell me about it. It might be the death of all of us."

They enter the stairway and start going upward. Bertha and Auntie become slightly winded as they reach the top of the second floor landing and start walking down the hallway toward Auntie's apartment through the dim lighting while carrying heavy bags. They reach Auntie's apartment and Auntie starts fumbling with a key trying to fit it into the lock. Bertha bends to place her package on the floor. She began to feel pain building up in her stomach. With one hand, she places it over her stomach, hiding her feeling from Auntie. Auntie is still working the key as she keeps twisting and turning it with an effort to make it fit into the hole. Auntie says without looking in Bertha's direction. "These keys are a mess. It hurts my fingers sometime trying to make this key work." Bertha manages to straighten up and down tone the sign of pain she is feeling on her face and in her body. "Auntie, let me do that for you."

Auntie gives up and hands her a key. "My eyes aren't what they use to be," she says. "Especially in this bad lighting. I tell you. They need to do something about these problems we been having around here. People taking the bulbs from the hallway to use in their own apartment. I don't know what these people gonna do next. Somebody could walk up behind me in this bad lighting and hurt me."

"You're right." Bertha mildly answers.

They enter the apartment. "Just sit the package on the kitchen table," she tells Bertha. "I been living here for as long as I can remember. No good ever comes with living here. It's tough on me carrying these bags up here. Sometimes I have to pay kids to carry them because I get out of breath as you can see. Old age is starting to take a toll on us older folks and I can see I ain't as well or fit as I use to be."

"Auntie, you doing good. You can still get out of bed in the morning and walk up and down those steps. And as far as those steps are concerned, I know what you mean. I been having to carry stuff up three flights of stairs myself and with my condition. It ain't no joke."

Auntie looks at Bertha. "What condition is that?"

"Sometimes I get these sharp pains in my stomach that last for just a few minutes."

"Tell me about it. I've been getting these pains in my legs from going up them steps, too. But don't worry about me. Take care of yourself."

"If you don't mind, can we sit a while? I want to tell you a little story about my childhood."

"Sure. We can sit in the front room after I finish putting these things away. She opened the refrigerator to see it was mostly filled. "They should give me a larger one. I need to store more food in here when some days I can't get out."

"Let me tell you something about these refrigerators."

Bertha helped with packing the frig and they went to sit in the front room near each other.

Bertha placed her hands close to her stomach in case the pain started up again. "I know you can think back to the old days when we didn't have all these modern things we have today. What I remember as a little girl was the ice man coming through the years carrying loads of block ice in an old truck. During the summer days, us kids would try to get under the truck so the ice water would drip on us. It was cold and fun."

"Wasn't you afraid of getting hurt under there?"

"No. The guy on the back of the truck would run us away just before the truck started moving. Anyway, in those days, there were no refrigerators in people's homes. Everybody had an icebox to keep their food cold."

"I remember that quite well. Sometime I got a block too large for my ice box. I had to chop off pieces to make it fit."

"We use to do the same thing. All I know is that as the block of ice melted, water would drip into a water pan just under the block. One day somebody forget to empty the pan and as I opened the icebox, water started pouring out ALL over the floor. I got scared and ran out of the house. I can laugh about it now. But back then, I learned to keep my mouth shut."

"I'm glad that was back then," said Auntie. "I would hate to be dealing with that mess at this age with little or no help. Especially since I have a problem with lifting heavy objects."

"And speaking of something cold," Bertha continued to speak. "There was an ice cream factory about a block away from where we lived. During the summer, I guess the factory was over producing. A truck would come through the neighborhood passing out free small packs of three flavored ice cream. And as I think back, that was the only time I can remember ever getting ice cream. People definitely could not keep it in their icebox."

Auntie started to laugh. "What a mess you could have had on your hands with the ice and the ice cream melting at the same time. You were right to keep your mouth shut. And you were lucky. I never got anything like that. I lived in the country on a farm. We were lucky enough just to get ice."

"I guess we got it because the factory was in our area. I use to play outside all day just waiting for that ice cream truck to come around the corner."

"How can you remember all this?"

"It's funny that you ask that. I guess when you're young, your brain is in good working order. As we grow older, some cells die causing our short-term memory as they say, 'stop working.' So, when you sometimes tell me you can't remember what happened five minutes ago, you said it right."

"I like that little story. You must come back again and tell me another one. I like old memories."

Bertha felt pleased. But she knew she had to make a stop at home. "Do you need any more help with anything?"

"No thank you. A nice girl like you should do yourself a favor and get away from here as soon as possible. This place is too dangerous for anybody. They don't bother me because I won't take any mess from them."

Bertha started thinking to herself. *'The reason no one bothers her is because she is crazy Flash's Aunt and Flash was not the type of person for you to be on the wrong side of. And people know that someday when Flash is released, they will be catching hell from him.'* I'm okay. I used to live here before. I know what's what and most of the people around here. It's getting near to the time for me to be going to work."

"Thanks again for the help. See your way out and pull the door shut tight. Sometimes it sticks and is hard to close."

Bertha entered her third-floor apartment. Drops her keys on a small table beside the door. The apartment looked both tidy and chaotic. Makeshift items being used as storage space spread around parts of the apartment. Aged wallpaper peeling from the walls and clutter is scattered here and there.

Breeze has busied himself watching cartoons on the television set while sitting on the couch directly in front of it.

"Hey Breeze." Bertha calls out.

Breeze shows no interest in her. His focus is trained on watching the set. He laughs at the action and makes a quick remark to her. "Hey," without taking his eyes from the set.

She walked toward the kitchen while saying to Breeze, "I'm sorry I'm late. Did you defrost the chicken like I asked ….." Bertha sees food all laid out on the dining room table ready to eat. "Did Mark cook?"

Breeze takes his eyes from the set to give a hard stare in her direction. "No. I did. He's not here. I don't like it when you use his name around me."

Bertha looked surprise. "Sorry I…."

Suddenly the apartment door opens. Mark walks in. Loudly he chuckles. "Hey Baby!" And walks over to kiss her on the cheek and ignores Breeze. Then heads toward the dining room table. He takes a plate and grabs a serving for himself. "Looks good. Somebody did a great job on fixing this. I can see we got somebody with food skills in the house."

"Breeze did it." She smiles at Breeze. "Maybe someday he might want to open a food place of his own."

Breeze looks in his mom's direction. "No way. Too much work."

Mark says, "Hire people and supervise them."

Breeze goes back to viewing the television without making any further comments.

Bertha comes to the table and fixes herself a plate. She looks at Breeze still watching television. "Breeze, honey, come sit down with us."

"I already ate." He replies without turning away from the set.

How Mark met Bertha. Mark was a good friend of Marcus who was Bertha's boyfriend before he ended up in prison. He had been seeing the two of them hanging out together. Marcus was always saying what a great person Bertha was. Mark had always wanted to hook up with her, but when she left town, he thought that was the end of that. It just so happened that one day when he was out and about running around trying to keep an eye on one of his two women, Dee Dee, who was working the streets, he saw Bertha going into a store. He when in and introduced himself to her and told her they had a friend in common, Marcus. This caught her attention. He asked if he could set up a day and time to take her out to dinner, she gladly accepted. At dinner, they started talking about things in common and soon became friends. He started going to her apartment where he met Breeze. Breeze knew Mark from the streets and didn't care for him being he was known by many to be a pimp and hustler. Breeze tried telling his mom about Mark's activities, but she didn't want to hear it. And so, Bertha and Mark's relationship began. Mark would come to Bertha's apartment at times and cook and help with her various needs. This was something that made Bertha like Mark even more.

Mark spent many nights with Bertha. He found out about her medical condition from hearing her crying out during the night in pain. He asked her about it but never received a satisfactory answer. So, he stopped asking. He tried asking Breeze about it. Breeze didn't know and asked Mark not to mention it to him again being he had a disliking for Mark.

Bertha goes to work early the next day. She had been doing such a good job that she was about to have her own customers. One of them entered the salon and Bertha directed her to her chair. She began working on the customer's hair while the customer started reading a magazine. Soft music played throughout the salon alone with some people having a soft conversation. It had seemed like a wonderful day working in the salon.

Mark has been having problems with Linda whom he was pimping and she was coming up short on cash that he needed to pay off a debt owed to a thug named

Trashman. He decided to keep an eye on her to see how much she was actually making. He had come to fear Trashman. Trashman was the type of guy that didn't play or ask questions when it came to paying back money owed to him. He got his name from trashing and wasting people even to a point of murdering them. Mark knew Trashman would soon be coming to collect on a debt. In the meantime, he decided to go out looking for Bertha and grab some money from her as a backup. He started out by going to the salon. He peeked through the glass door. He sees her working and goes inside and straight up to her working area. All the workers and customers eyes followed him. Most of them know him from the streets. Mark stops next to Bertha's chair. She doesn't see him. Her back is turned toward him while she is working.

"Can I talk to you?" He asked in a low voice.

Bertha quickly turns to face him startled. "What are you doing here? Can't you see I'm working?"

"I just wanted to see you. I won't stay long."

Bertha's co-worker sneers at him and some of the others in salon give him a dirty look from their work station. By now, Bertha is starting to ware an exasperated look on her face because she knows she's been down this road before with him about money. So she knew the real deal. She whispers to him, "How much do you need this time?" And she backs away.

"Mark moves in close and whispers into her ear. "A couple hundred dollars."

She looks around to see who is watching her. They all are. She takes out her wallet. Counts out ten twenties. Extends them to him. "Here. Take this. This is all can spare."

Mark whispers, "Thanks Baby, Bye." He kisses her on her forehead and leaves. Her co-worker rolls her eyes and says, "Street trash. Good for nothing. I wouldn't give him the time of day. You a better woman then I am."

Feeling out of place, Bertha is apologetic to the women. "I'm really sorry about that."

The lady in her chair looks in the mirror at Bertha. "Child, you and me both." She goes back to reading her magazine and the other women start to mumble between themselves.

Mark's apartment is dimly lit with barely any light peeking through the dark curtains. Beer cans, beer bottles and plastic wrappers liter the floor. On a makeshift coffee table are the two hundred dollars he received from Bertha.

Seeing Mark is a less then middle-aged man without his t-shirt. He sports a prominent tattoo of a snake eating its own tail on his arm while he is sitting on a couch. Beside him is Linda, a young lady dressed in very tight clothing and Dee Dee is in the bathroom.

Linda hands to him a fist full of dollars she made while hustling out on the streets. He adds her money to what is on the table and takes a small wad from his pocket to add to his collection. Smiling, he looks up at her. "Baby, you did good. Just need for you to make a little more. I hope Dee Dee is doing as good as you. Hey Dee Dee. Hurry out of the bathroom. I need some money from you."

She calls out. "Don't be rushing me. I'll be there when I'm finished."

Linda places her hand on Mark's leg. "Ain't I your number one girl?"

"Yeah baby. Number one."

She takes her hand from his leg and starts playing with his hair with one hand and trying to look sexy while stroking at him sensually with the other. She whispers into his ear. "Why don't you take a break and have a little fun with me." Mark removed the smile on his face. "I can't right now. Get business to take care of." She starts nibbling on his ear. "Stop!" He tells her. She pays no attention to him. He pushes her off the couch. She lands on some of the trash scattered around the floor. He gives her a mean look. "Don't mean to be mean. Just stay off me. I don't want to spoil our business relationship."

"SERIOUSLY?" She shot back at him and moves to stand on her feet. Her clothes are partly trashed.

She began brushing herself off and fixing her hair. "I thought you thought better of me. Now I know you have no respect for me. What am I to you? A good lay providing cash for you? You just said I was your number one girl. And now you dumping on me. You are probably treating me the same way you're treating that witch Dee Dee."

Mark scoffs at her. "You should be grateful. You'd be dead if I didn't pick you up from the streets."

Dee Dee comes from the bathroom. "What's this I hear somebody calling me a witch. I ain't gon'na be too many of them. You messing with the wrong person."

"Dee Dee I need the money you made." She gets her purse and takes out a wad of bill. "Keep a hundred for yourself and fork over the rest." She gives him a crazy look like you must be crazy. "Here." She throws it all to him. He tries to catch it as it spreads out in front of him.

"Don't be hating." He picks it all up and places one hundred of the money near the edge of the table for her. She doesn't take it. He stares at her for a moment and goes back to concentrating as he continues counting money and doing quick math while mumbling to himself.

Linda folds her arm across her breast while staring down at him.

He feels her presence and can see her feet up close to him. Without looking up, he says to her. "Make yourself useful. Clean up some of this mess."

Linda walked away, finds a broom and dustpan and returns to Mark who is still sitting and handling money. Spitefully she says, "Make me. This is your mess. Didn't your mama teach you how to clean up after yourself?"

Dee Dee breaks out into laughter. Mark stops counting. He stands to look Linda straight into her eyes. He slapped her face and grabbed a fistful of hair on top of her head and pulls down hard on it. She flinches in pain. Dee Dee rushes over to him and grabs one of his arms. "You hit her again and I'll hurt you."

He becomes furious. "Don't give me that stupid attitude. I see the both of you been taking some of my money and I don't like it. I could finish the both of you off and nobody would even notice you're gone."

Dee Dee releases his arm. "Oh. You think you that bad. You ain't seen me in action. The last guy who tried to do something to me is pushing up daisies."

Mark let go of Linda by pushing her backwards. "For a minute you two were doing good. But now the both of you are acting stupid. GET OUT! Go make me some more money. And don't come back until you have something to give to me."

Linda throws the broom and dustpan on the floor at his feet. Both ladies walk out the door with Linda being the last person, slamming it hard behind her.

Mark signs. "Finally, some peace. What a real nut job I got on my hands dealing with the two of them."

Suddenly there's knocking on the door. Mark groans. Annoyed. "What now. I sure hope it ain't them." The knocks get louder. "Cool it. I'm coming." He puts away the money and goes to the door. Upon opening it, he comes face to face with Breeze. Furiously, he rushes in and stops in the middle of the floor. Mark looks confused. With trembling lips, Breeze bellows out. "Stay away from my mom. You. Bad news. She…"

Mark cuts him off. "You don't tell me who I should be seeing. She likes me and there is nothing you can do about it. Get out of here before I hurt you."

"And if you hurt my mom." He sticks a finger into Mark's face. "Just don't. Because you WILL see the other side of me."

Mark flares up. Smacks Breeze's hand away and points a finger toward the door. "Out of here. And when I come to her pad, you better treat me with respect. GET OUT NOW! Before I show you what I can do to you."

"OH? You think you bad?"

Mark walks to the door and opens it. He waves his hand for Breeze to leave.

Breeze starts walking toward the door. "Just remember who I am." He exits and walks away.

The next day, Bertha returned to the salon to do her regular working routine. While working she touches her stomach and winces in pain. Her co-worker happened to take notice. "Are you okay?" She asked. Bertha now begins to hold her stomach with both hands. "Yeah. I'm okay." She replied after noticing other ladies looking in her direction. She goes to the ladies room, downs two of her pills and returns. She goes back to work with a grimace look on her face obviously still in slight pain.

Monique, curvy, curly hair longtime girlfriend lay on Bertha's couch smoking a marijuana joint. Bertha sits in her favorite spot by the kitchen window looking down at the parking lot below. She watches as people are coming and going. With an unpleasant look on her face, she tells Monique, "I came back here thinking life would be different, but I see it's not. We got a new mayor that turned his back on the people living here. Gangs still causing problems and tenants doing their own thing. To me, it looks like the drug dealers are having a ball. Cars by the dozen are coming into the parking lot and drug dealers are running wild to meet them."

Monique repositioned herself on the couch. She takes a long drag from her joint, holds it partly in while trying to speak. "Girlfriend, you know I've been here a long time and every day to me seems to be the same. If it wasn't for me being able to get as much marijuana as I want from people I know, I'd move tomorrow." Monique gets up from the couch and staggers to the kitchen table to hand Bertha the joint. Bertha starts to feel a sudden pain coming back. She slightly eases her hand over the pain area trying not to let Monique know what's going on. She takes the joint reluctantly, takes a quick puff, coughs and passes it back. Still holding her stomach, she manages to say, "I'm good." She lies and turns back to looking out the window only to see small kids running around the grounds with no parents in sight. The pain passes and she is back to her old self. "Those kids playing, and nobody watching. That's how that little boy got shot in the sandbox before I left here years ago."

Monique takes a puff of her joint. "A lot of the older people here say they are scared of this gang who keep coming around here causing trouble. I have no problems with them. Other people like visitors coming around here say they are afraid of them also. They say Trashman is creating the most serious problems around. People are afraid to turn him in because he got boy watching his back. The last person who called the police on him is still in the hospital. And that was about two weeks ago."

Bertha fans at the smoke Monique has blown toward her. "I do know. This place is falling apart. Outside and inside. It's a mess all over." She sits for a moment thinking. "I need to get me and Breeze out of this rat trap. The way you are talking, this guy, Trashman and his boys might do something to Breeze since he likes hanging around in that courtyard."

"I wouldn't doubt it."

Breeze walks alone as he enters the Miller Homes area. Candyman, a short gangster looking thug obviously under the influence of something is following Breeze. He calls out to Breeze. "Hey. Homey." Breeze ignores him and walks a little faster. Candyman speeds up his pace to catch up as they walk side by side. Breeze is starting to show signs of being a little nervous. "I think you got the wrong guy." Breeze tries to shake him off. Candyman is persistent. "We could use a dude like you." They stop walking. Breeze looks him straight into his eyes with a slight loud panic in his voice. "I'm not your homey and I sure ain't a dude. My name is Breeze. You got that. And I'm not interested in what you got to say."

"Hey, chill Breeze. Don't get up tight. I only had something to offer." Candyman discreetly takes out a small business card. "Think about it."

Breeze looks down at the card while Candyman is writing something on it. Breeze looks up. Candyman is still writing. "I know what you're all about. I ain't into a gangster style life." Candyman looks up. "You got me all wrong. This is all business." He hands Breeze the card. Breeze reads over the writing. *'Paper route job is open if you want it.'* He becomes confused and looks around for Candyman. Just that fast, he is nowhere to be seen.

Candyman had been watching the Miller Homes area for a long time before Sonny Bee and Flash's gang were removed. Shortly after their arrest, he seen the opportunity to move his operation from the streets into Miller Homes where the real action existed. But as time moved forward, he found himself faced with competition. Trashman, who is a force not to be reckoned with is making it difficult to conduct business in this area. He decided he would deal with Trashman when the need becomes necessary.

Bertha was checking into work holding her stomach with sweat heavily brewing around her lips. Her co-worker standing behind her is waiting to check in as well. Suddenly, Bertha passes out onto the floor. Her co-worker immediately locates her cell phone and dials 911. The medics arrived in a short period of time and roll Bertha away.

At the hospital, Bertha lay on a bed in a public ward. Breeze walks into the hospital wearing a worried expression on his face. He checks in with a doctor who gives him the bad news. He immediately goes to his mom's room. Minutes later, Mark appears placid. Breeze and Mark both knows about the pain Bertha is in. Only Breeze knows what is causing it.

"How bad is it?" Mark asked.

Breeze holds back for a moment wondering if he should tell him. Suddenly he blurts out. "It's cancer! That's what the doctor is saying."

Mark becomes frustrated and sadly pinches his temple. "Cancer? Jesus Christ how will we manage this situation?"

Breeze holds his mother's hand and looks down at her with tears in his eyes and her eyes are half opened. He says to her in almost a whisper. "You'll be okay. Right mom?"

She manages to look up at him. "Of course. Sweetie. Stop crying. It can be fixed."

Mark becomes angry. Son of a …" He is quick to catch himself and stops as he sees a lady doctor coming in, in the middle of his sentence. She brings with her a clip board. Immediately she walks to Bertha's side. Breeze and Mark back away from the bed. "How are you feeling?" she asked. Bertha has a half smile on her face. "It could be worse." Doctor looks at Mark. "Are you the husband?"

Breeze perks up at hearing her speak. Angrily he shouts "NO! He's my mom's boyfriend."

The Doctor looks at Breeze and raises her eyebrows. "Are the both of you living with her?"

Mark tells the Doctor. "Yeah, I guess you could say so. I live around there part time." He points toward Breeze. "He lives there."

The Doctor takes a quick examination of Bertha while the two watch. She then hands several pieces of papers to Breeze. She starts to explain what is needed. "These are items and treatment Bertha…." Breeze is looking at his mother who is listening to the conversation, but his head is not with the Doctor. Somehow, he is wondering how he can help his mom.

Mark walks up to the Doctor. Gently speaking. "We got this. Thank you, Doctor." The Doctor looks at him strangely. "I beg your pardon. I'm the Doctor around here. This is worse than you can imagine. She needs real help. And how do you got this?" Mark doesn't speak. "She needs to start treatment immediately. We will keep her here while we start her first treatment. Then she will have to come in monthly. Hopefully, we can cure her." She stares at him for a another silent moment and walks out the room. Breeze reads over some of the list out loud. Besides being ill, Bertha is worried and desperate. "How are we possibly going to be able to afford these cost?"

Mark, tell her. "We'll find a way baby. Don't worry."

The sound of the conversation drowns out as Breeze stares into blankness.

Several days later, Bertha is released from the hospital. She is placed into a taxi along with Breeze and Mark. They arrived at Miller Homes and she is helped into her apartment. After getting settled in, Mark takes Breeze into the kitchen so Bertha is not able to hear their conversation. He starts by saying in a low voice, "I need to talk to you about your mom." Breeze starts walking away. "There's nothing you can tell me. I can't stand to even be around you. Leave." Mark grabs him by the arm as Breeze starts to pass before him. "No.

Seriously. You need to listen." Breeze stops, looks down at Mark is holding him arm. "Get off me." Breeze starts walking again. This time toward the front door.

Mark is following him still holding onto his arm. "Do you really want to help your mom?"

Breeze stops. "Let my arm go. What do you mean?"

Mark complies. "A business opportunity."

Breeze has been working his 9 to 5 job for the past 3 Months in an office building in the center of town. The pay isn't all that great. With his mom's medical bills coming up, he is thinking about getting a second job. He thought about the paper route. But he turned his thought away because delivering papers doesn't pay a lot. Starting tomorrow, he would be out looking in other areas for work.

Mark had other ideas about helping Breeze make some quick money. Also though Breeze didn't care for Candyman, this would be Breeze's best to cover his mom's needs.

Mark takes Breeze to Candyman's apartment. Breeze shows a signs of being surprised when he sees Candyman. He remembered him from the meeting near the parking lot. Breeze has lost his fear of Candyman after being with Mark. "I know him and what he's all about." Mark is surprised. Breeze takes the business card from his worn-out wallet. Mark takes the card, looks it over, and looks Candyman straight into his face. "So, you two met before?"

"Yeah," says Candyman. "We been seeing each other around." He gives Breeze the once over look. "You ever heard of the paper route around here?"

"Yeah, I don't know. Not sure," talking out of confusion.

Candyman looked at Mark and raised an eyebrow. Then returned his attention to Breeze. "If you want'ta work for me, it's a simple job. All you gotta do is deliver the newspaper. Pick up the cash. No questions asked. Got it?"

Surprised. Breeze repeated it so he doesn't get a miss understanding. "Deliver the papers. Pick up the cash. No questions asked. I think I can do that. How much does it pay?"

"A hundred bucks and more for a few hours a day's work. That's if you go out."

"And how many days a week will I be going out?"

"Every day if you like. It's a job. You can't be messing around. I don't play that. You interested?"

"Sounds good. I'll try it and see if it works for me."

"You will be delivering in Tower One. Let me give you a list of stops." He walks away to his bedroom and returned with a list of addresses, hands it to Breeze to go over. Breeze is thinking real money. Surprised at what he will receive. Can't get it out of his head. "Deliver the papers. Pick up the cash. No questions asked. Sounds easy enough."

"Try it for a day and if you like it, I'll put you on."

"Solid."

Breeze is so excited that he is chatting the words in delight all the way to Bertha's apartment. "Deliver the papers. Pick up the cash. No questions asked. Deliver the papers. Pick up the cash. No questions asked. Nice ring to it." Little does he know that somewhere down the line, these same words would lose there meaning.

CHAPTER
Three

Next morning Breeze wakes up early. He looks over the addresses and after washing up, getting dress and eating a little something. He goes to Candyman's apartment and picks up a stack of rolled up newspapers. He walks up to the tenth floor, knocks on a door. Waits. Not wanting to waste time, he knocks harder. A big man opens the door. Breeze extends the paper to him.

The big man hesitates to take the paper. He asked, "Are you the paper boy?"

"Yeah," replied Breeze.

Big man takes the paper and tells Breeze, "Wait here." He goes off leaving the door slightly opened. A few minutes pass and the man returned with an envelope that he passes off to Breeze.

"Thanks," Breeze replied. He thinks to himself. *This is easy. He was right. No problems.*' He started working his way down to the next level. He knocks at the next address on the list. A small kid opens the door. Breeze looks down at him. "Get your mom or dad." The kid runs off leaving the door wide open. In the background Breeze can hear a man saying, "Boy! Don't be opening that door. You don't know who might be out there." A minute later, the man comes to the door looking mean and growls at Breeze. "What you want?"

Breeze feels nervous trying to wear a straight face. "I come to deliver your newspaper." The man says, "Wait here." He goes off and quickly returns with the money. Still no questions asked. On the next level down, a middle-aged lady comes to the door but does not open it. She looks through the peep hold. Breeze can see movement on the other side. He hears a strange voice saying, "Que?" (Spanish word for what). Breeze doesn't understand but replied "Paper Boy."

The voice on the other side asked, "Paper?"

"Paper," he repeats himself.

"Oh, Paper." She opened the door part way to reveal half of herself. She appears to be Spanish. "Que?" Comes from her mouth again.

He shows her the newspaper.

"No speakey English."

He pulls out a dollar bill from his pocket and points at the dollar and newspaper back and forth.

She eyes him for a moment. "Oh. OK." Then she disappears into the apartment.

While waiting, he hears funny talking in the apartment.

A Spanish looking man comes to the door and hands Breeze the money in exchange for the paper and he leaves. Going down to the next three flights of stairs, he passes an opened door and sees a family living in a cramped space in the background. He sees many kids and very little living space. He feels very bad for them. This was his first time seeing how very poor people can really live. He hopes his future will never come to this.

Breeze completed the route just in time to catch a bus and head for work. At work, he made himself comfortable behind his desk thinking about the cash he collected this morning. He was wondering if the money he was making from Candyman would be more then what his job was paying him. If so, he would quit working at his low paying job and do the papers to have more free time and make more money at the same time. This would depend on how many papers Candyman would let him deliver. He would have to rap to him the next time they meet up to give him the money and get paid.

That evening after work, Breeze goes straight to Candyman's apartment. He only had to knock once before Candyman opened the door with a mean look about him. "What took you so long to get here. I thought you skipped town. Come on in and where's my money?"

Breeze takes from his pocket the bills and envelopes, hands them to Candyman. Breeze is the type of person to get nervous quick. And knowing the kind of repetition Candyman has, Breeze became nervous quickly. "Nobody asked and I didn't say I had a job. I finished delivering the papers just in time to catch the bus for work."

Candyman calms down. "My bad. I didn't give it a thought. We okay." He counted the money. Smiled as he looked up at Breeze while handing him a one-hundred-dollar bill. "This is for you. Nice work."

Breeze is shocked into happiness. "All this for one hour delivering papers?"

"Yeah. Don't let this go to your head. There's a lot more from where this came from. He taps on Breeze's shoulder and lightly pushes him toward the door. "Get out of here. See you in the morning."

Still in shock. "Thanks."

Candyman slammed the door close behind Breeze leaving.

As Breeze is walking toward home, his thoughts return to the money. *That's not a bad job. I could use the money to help mom with her medical bills. Yeah! I think I could quit my job if I can deliver a lot more papers, for sure. I'm gonna rap to Candyman about getting more deliveries.*

Breeze meets two guys coming into the courtyard. Bill and Buck are just a little older then him. As the two walk closer toward Breeze, they stop Breeze. "Hey," says Bill. "You the new paper boy, right?"

"Yeah. How'd you know?"

"Please. I know everything that goes on with Candyman's life. Besides, I saw you carrying a load of papers this morning just after I came from Candyman's crib."

"Are you guys paper boys too?"

Bill lights a cigarette. "We used to be."

"So, you don't work for him anymore?"

"We do."

"What's Candyman letting you guys do?"

"Samething you do just up front."

Breeze looked confused. "I don't get it."

Bill and Buck laugh. "Man, you really don't know what you're getting yourself into, huh?"

Bill takes a long drag on his cigarette and looks at buck in a surprising way of showing Breeze that something is going on that he should be knowing. He hands the cigarette to Buck who places it into his mouth. "You're selling dope in those papers."

Breeze becomes surprised. "What? No way."

"Please," says Bill. "Don't be surprised. You wouldn't be talking and working for Candyman if you weren't desperate for money. "

"Nah man. I'm just doing the papers."

"Be real. Do you think you can be making that kind of money just delivering newspapers?"

Bill has Breeze thinking.

"See for yourself." Bill unfolds a newspaper he is holding to reveal drugs tucked inside. Breeze stares at it. "What. No way." He looks horrified and runs into Tower One.

Breeze makes his way up to Bertha's apartment panting. Mark is watching television. "Where's mom?" breeze asked between breathing heavily.

"Sleeping."

"You didn't tell me I was dealing dope." Breeze shoves Mark. Mark stands and pushes him back. Mark puts his right finger to his lips. "Shhh." He whispers. "You'll wake her. You think you can make that kind of money on that low paying job working in an office? Your mom is sick, and you need to do everything you can to help her out." Mark can see he has captured Breeze's attention. "Now you got to keep your mouth shut and do the route. Remember, you're doing this for her. I just want you to always remember this. Your mom birth you. She changed your diapers. Feed you. Bought you clothes. Took care of you while you was growing up. Made sure you got an education. Took you wherever she went. Gave you what you needed when she did without for herself. And gave you advice when you needed it. That's a mother's love. She ain't asking nothing in return. You owe her. Now is the time to show her love with all the support you can give to her. If I had a mom like yours, I'd jump out the window for her if she asked me to. My mom didn't do all those things for me. She turned me loose to the streets. Your Dad. What did he ever do for you except help bring you into this mean world. When was the last time you saw or heard from him?. I ain't saying he's a bad guy. All I'm saying, he ain't there for you. I ain't gonna say nothing more about this subject."

Breeze started feeling bad after hearing from Mark. He doesn't say a word. Just walks out the door from the apartment.

The next morning, Breeze skips work. He is just finishing the paper route and heads for Candyman's apartment where Bill lets him in after several knocks. The room is quiet. He hands Candyman the money he collected from the route. Candyman counts it quickly. Impressed. "9 Gs. Nice. Not bad. Anyone giving you a hard time?"

"No. Everything's cool. Everything went just as you told me. Deliver the papers. Pick up the cash. No questions asked."

"Good. I'm glad you got it."

Bill takes a seat on the couch and smiles. Candyman gets up and pats both of them on the back. "Good. Good. Boss Man will be bringing more papers tomorrow." He puts the money into a duffel bag and takes it into his bedroom. Calling from the bedroom. "Hey, Bill. Why don't you grab a couple of beers from the fridge?"

Bill stands, goes into the kitchen. Opens the fridge. The fridge is mostly filled with beers. He takes out three cans.

Candyman strolls back into the common area and slumps himself onto the couch. Bill hands him a beer and sits on the couch while turning on the television. Bill keeps one for himself and places the other on a stand. Candyman grabs the remote from a nearby stand and starts flipping through the channels. He opens the can. It HISSES. He takes along chug and lights a cigarette and looks at Breeze who is standing right in front of them. He waves his hand at Breeze to move to one side so he can view the television. Candyman hands Breeze a can. Breeze looks at it then at Candyman.

Breeze becomes nervous. "UH. No thanks. Hey, can I get the cash? Got'ta bounce soon." He places the can on an end table.

Candyman looks at him with a frustrated look. He CLICKS his tongue. Then starts nudging Bill. "What's the matter? We too good for you Breeze?"

Bill nods. "Yeah! We too good for you? Lucky Candyman took you in. Ain't that right Candyman?" Bill pop's the tab and takes a swig from his beer.

Breeze is apologetic. "No. No. I just have to be somewhere."

Candyman raises his voice. "You good for nothing mooch. I tell you when you can leave." He slams the beer can on the table. Foam spills over the top of the can and down the side. Candyman stands and shoots Breeze a glare. Breeze stays quiet looking down at his feet, scared. Candyman laughs. "Just messing with you." He punches Breeze playfully on the shoulder. Then goes into his bedroom, reaches his hand down into the duffle bag, pulls out a stack of dollar bills. He goes back into the common room and walks up to Breeze. Breeze is a little nervous because he doesn't know what to expect. Candyman unfolds two, one hundred-dollar bills and place them into Breeze's hand.

Breeze feels relieved. "Thanks."

Candyman smiles at him. "Take care, kid. Don't forget to come tomorrow."

Breeze starts to feel nervous again. "I'll be here."

Candyman slumps back onto the couch.

Breeze and Bill walk out of the apartment together. Bill can feel what Breeze is thinking. "He likes you and that's a good sign."

"I don't know. He scares me."

"Don't be afraid of him. He may act tough, but he has a soft heart. You work for him long enough and you'll see."

They separate. Breeze walks down the sidewalk heading towards home. He stops at the same candy store he did years ago. He goes into the candy and junk food isle looking for a chocolate bar. Confused because there are so many, he grabs the smallest one from a rack and brings it to the cashier. She stands from her stool where she had just finished filing her nails and is smacking wildly on gum she's been chewing. "That'll be a $1.50." Her eyes move around quickly as if not paying attention to the transaction.

Breeze stares at her. He hesitates to give her the money. "It was $1.00 last week."

She looks at him sarcastically. "You want it or not?"

Breeze is not pleased. He takes one of the bills and hands it to her.

She looks at him. "You trying to be funny? You giving me this bill for a $1.50 candy bar?"

"Yeah. I need the change. You got a problem with that?"

She takes the bill and stares at it. Holds it up to the light. Not detecting any problems, she runs the bill through an ultraviolet money scanner under the counter. It cleared. She punches digits into the register. Breeze watches her. She looks mean. "Don't think you're getting a bag for this." She hands him the bar. "You want tens?" Breeze nods yes. "Here." She places the money into his hand and he starts walking toward the door. "Dumb broad. The owners needs to hire someone with brains," he says.

"I heard that. We don't need your business. Spending $1.50. Don't come back. You hear me?"

"You better believe it. I won't." And he walks out of the store.

Breeze finally arrived at home. Bertha is in the kitchen and comes out to greet him. He hands her the money. " Where did you get this money from?" She ask surprisingly.

Mark is sitting on the couch. "Kid's a hard worker. Does the newspaper route as a side J-O-B."

Bertha seems pleased. "Look at you. Working two jobs." She kisses him on the cheek.

Breeze goes to his job the next morning. He doesn't check in. Instead, he goes straight to his Boss' office. The Boss has not arrived. He takes a seat behind his desk and writes a note. "This is from Breeze. I quit. Send my check to my home. Bye." He places it in the center of the desk so his Boss wouldn't miss it and walked out the door.

Breeze does his route with no problems and goes immediately to Candyman's apartment to give the money he's collected and get paid. He thinks this would be a good time to ask Candyman about adding more papers to his route. He knocked once. Bill opened the door.

Candyman has made himself comfortable on the couch. He waves his hand toward Breeze. "Come on in and cop a squat."

Breeze comes in and takes a seat next to him. With all the money in his hand, he hands it to Candyman who counts it. Then counts out three one, one-hundred-dollar bills and hands them to Breeze.

Breeze has a worried look on his face.

Candyman takes notice. "What's up Breeze?" He asked.

"My mom's sick. And I need money to help with the medical bills. I was wondering if you could increase my route?"

"Yeah. No problem. Okay." Candyman goes into his bedroom and returned with two list. He hands them to Breeze, who takes a quick look at them and smiles.

"These okay with you?"

"Yeah. I can do this."

"Be here in the morning to get the papers."

"Thanks, Candyman." Breeze stands and heads out the apartment.

The next morning Breeze collects the papers from Candyman and starts his route. As he continues to work his way down to the bottom floor, several of the customers in Tower One are not answering the door. He is forced to hold onto the few papers before a delivery through Tower Two. At this point, he decides to run down to the drug store and pick up some of mom's meds. Along the way, two guys see him and follow him to the store. Breeze goes inside while the two guys wait outside. A short time later, he comes out. The two guys approach him in a manner that prevented him from walking away. One guy reaches out to take his papers. Breeze draws the papers close to his body. One of them asked. "What you got there?"

Breeze hesitates to answer. "Newspapers. Why you ask?"

"We want them."

"Look. I got'ta bounce. They ain't for sale."

The other guy steps up close to Breeze to get in his face. "Oh. You must be the new paper boy."

"Yeah. What's it to you?"

"You moving in on our territory?"

Breeze begins to feel a little uncomfortable. "No. Just passing through."

"If you come back here again and we see you, we gonna have something for you. Now we gonna be taking those papers. If you like it or not."

"Not if I can help it. IF you do, you better be ready to deal with Candyman."

They laugh. One of them says, "Candyman is a punk and if he don't watch himself, we gonna take him out."

"You don't know Candyman." They reach for the papers again. He panics and pushes his way through them and starts running off still holding tight to the papers. The two guys start running after him. In a short distance away they stop. Breeze makes a turn at the corner and runs out of sight.

A short time later, Breeze arrives at Miller Homes. He finishes the paper route and as he is walking through the courtyard, he hears this "HUNK. HUNK." He looks for the sound and sees Candyman sitting in his BMW parked by the curb. Buck is sitting in the back passenger seat. He waves for Breeze to come to the car. He calls out, "Get in." With urgency in his voice, he calls out again. "Hurry up!"

Breeze reluctantly is confused as he walks toward the car. "What's up?" Buck opens the back door and Breeze jumps in. He hands today's collection up front to Candyman, who immediately starts counting it. Bill, who is sitting in the front seat slurs out to Breeze. "You trying to get yourself killed?"

"What do you mean?" Breeze ask still looking confused.

"We saw you with them two dudes at the med store."

"Oh." Breeze become unconfused. "They were interested in getting a paper. I told them they wasn't for sale."

"They were some of Trashman's boys. You walking around in enemy territory with papers? If they spot you again with any papers, you might be dead meat."

"Sorry. I didn't know I was in their territory."

Candyman took a cigarette from his mouth and looked at Breeze through the rearview mirror. "So, you met the enemy! Trashman's gang."

Buck was quick to say, "We need to stop them from putting fear into our people."

"He's right," said Bill. "We don't go around there. It's too dangerous. We keep our business in the Miller Homes area."

Breeze looks puzzled. "I realize now that I was out of my territory. But I was just going to get meds for my mom. These two goons stopped me. I didn't do or say anything to them that I was working in their area."

"You was carrying papers. It don't matter. That's what turned them on to you. If you leave the area, don't take any papers. You got that?"

"Yeah."

Bill speaks up. "It don't matter anymore. They know who you are and think what you are all about."

"I'll be careful."

Breeze and Buck climb out of the car and walk away. Candyman drives off.

Later, Candyman and Bill go cruising down the avenue. They spot a gangster looking guy exiting a nearby convenience store carrying two cases of beer. Candyman speaking in a low tone of voice. "Speaking of the Devil. That's one of them." The car speeds up and zooms pass the guy. Bill looks into his outside rearview mirror. "I don't think he saw us. He was walking kind of funny like. I think he must have had a few before he came for another supply."

"Good," says Candyman. "I'm tired of tiptoeing around these punks." He scoffed. "Just keep a lookout. Trashman is merciless. He might be around somewhere. If he catches you around here, you won't be around to tell us what happened when he gets finished with you. Maybe we should take those cases of beer." Candyman circles the block. By the time they return, the guy has disappeared.

They pick up Breeze who has just completed his route and the three go out for a joy ride. The stereo in the car is blasting and Bill is singing and rapping along with the lyrics. Breeze is displeased.

They drive through downtown. Bill spots a few of his home boys and waves to them while still singing out of toon. Candyman turns off the stereo. Bill stopped singing and gives him a mean look. "Why you do that? I was on a roll."

Candyman laughs. "I heard dogs making better noise than what you trying to do." Breeze laughs under his breath with one hand covering his mouth. Candyman begins to chatter about trivial things. Breeze isn't listening. He sinks into the car seat looking sad and withdrawn.

Trashman, pale, skin head with his gang stroll onto the Miller Homes courtyard. Candyman is standing next to Tower One talking with Bill and Buck. Mark is walking toward Trashman while looking down and counting a fistful of dollar bills. Breeze sees Mark in a distance and follows him being careful not to be seen. Trashman calls out to Mark. Mark looks up and sees Trashman and gang starting to walk in his direction. Candyman and his two boys catch wind of what's happening and go to join Trashman's group. Before Mark reaches Trashman, Candyman arrives first and is quick to get into Trashman's face. "Huh. Aren't you out of your territory?"

"I go where I want." Trashman shouted back. "Mark owes me and I came to collect. You got a problem with that?"

Mark reaches the group. Trashman is looking ugly. He tells Mark, "Give me my money." Mark counts out several hundred-dollar-bills and hands them to Trashman while Candyman looks at Mark. Trashman is also looking at Mark. Point blank Trashman says to Mark. "You're short." Candyman jumps into Trashman's face angrily. "You don't make deals on my turf." Trashman shoots back. "You better get out of my face you little piss ball." Candyman freaks out and starts punching Trashman in the face. Immediately, the two groups become engaged in battle. Trashman falls to the ground. Candyman rushes over to him and aims his pistol at him. Mark runs into Tower One. Breeze takes off running and starts to follows him. One of Candyman's gang members pulls out a pistol and fires two shots over their head. Breeze dives to the ground. People in the area run to avoid being struck by any stray bullets. The fighting stopped. Trashman manages to get onto his feet. Candyman is still pointing his pistol at Trashman. He wipes blood from his face with one hand and holds a balled fist in the other. "You know this is WAR! If we catch ANY of your punks in our territory, they can kiss life good-bye."

Candyman is not moved. "The same goes here. Now walk away while you can still stand before I pull this trigger."

Showing signs of deep madness, Trashman and his two gang members walk away. One of them looks back as they exit the grounds. "DEAD. DEAD. DEAD. All of you."

Breeze gets up from the ground and runs into Tower One. He enters Bertha's apartment. Mark is already there. He hands Breeze several dollars he has been holding back from Trashman. "Use this to help with your mom's bills."

Breeze takes the money without saying a word. Mark stares at him. "Aren't you going to say something?"

"Why should I. You know how I feel about you. Keep your eyes on me. I can't wait to show you my other side."

"You better come correct because I won't be playing with you either."

Bertha spends the day at the hospital receiving her treatment. Afterwards, she goes home to rest for the remainder of the day. The next day, she goes back to work. The place is packed with customer. It has been rough on her overnight since leaving the hospital. She is looking tired and feels weak while laying the edge of her customer's hair while the customer reads a magazine.

Breeze completed his route and is headed toward the drug store. Approaching the store, he looks around and doesn't see the two gang members, so he goes inside. After purchasing his mom's meds, he casually strolls back toward the glass door. The same two Trashman's gang members who previously spotted him going into the store come from across the street to wait by the door as he comes outside. Not suspecting to be greeted by any of Trashman's gang, Breeze comes out and immediately spots them.

The tall slender one stops him. "I see you didn't listen the last time us telling you this was our territory. Since you didn't understand anything we said, I got a little something for you." He pulled out a pistol and points it at Breeze's leg. "This is going to prove we mean business."

Breeze freezes.

BEEP. BEEP. BEEP. Bertha's cell phone has been ringing and still is. She stops working to look at the ID. It's Monique. Bertha declines the call. She goes back to fixing her customer's hair. The phone starts ringing again. She stops again to look at the ID. It's her again. She whispers to herself. *'Can't you see I'm working girl?'*

The customer in her chair is in no hurry to have her hair fixed. She says to Bertha politely, "Honey, just answer the phone. I don't mind." She goes back to reading the magazine. Bertha's hands are messy from working on the hair. She cleans them by wiping them on a towel. Smiles and answers the call. "Hey girl. What's up? I guess you know I'm at work. I can't talk long."

Monique is crying on the phone. "Come to the med store."

Bertha has lost the glow on her face. "Why. What's happening?"

Crying louder. "It's Breeze."

Bertha goes into shock. "What?"

Monique is still crying. "He's been shot."

"GIRL! MONIQUE! What on earth are you talking about?"

Everyone in the salon, now is looking at her.

Sounding pitiful, Monique blurs out. "Just come to the store…Please…"

Bertha is frozen listening to Monique crying at the other end of the line. Her co-worker is looking at her funny. The phone call leaves Bertha disoriented. "I need to leave. It's an emergency." She scrambles to get his bag and jacket and clutches them to her body.

Her co-worker is in shock. "Excuse me? Last time I checked you had a job here."

She runs out the door as if not hearing a word her co-worker said.

Her co-worker quickly goes to the door and called out to Bertha's back. "Where are you going? You ain't finished with your customer." Bertha pretends she still doesn't hear her and keeps on going. Her co-worker comes back into the shop. "That girl's a mess. I don't know what I'm going to do with her." Bertha's customer is feeling funny sitting in the chair with no one to work on her hair. She turns to the co-worker. "What now?"

The police surround the drug store crime scene. A crowd of people gather around the police line. Bertha spots Monique talking to one of the officers. The officer is taking notes from her. Monique sees Bertha as she is walking toward her.

Bertha says to Monique, "What happened?"

Monique hugs Bertha tight. "The police are questioning people in an effort to figure out who did it."

Bertha moved away from Monique and moved through a crowd and pass a tape surrounding a small pool of blood. She sees Breeze laying on the concrete sidewalk. She gasps. Tears well up in her eyes. "BREEZE! NO HONEY! BREEZE!"

Breeze had been shot on the side of his leg. The medics are working on him. He sees her and speaks in a low voice. "Mom, calm down. It's not that bad. I can still move around."

Not able to think, she speaks out of her head. "No baby. You're hurt and need medical attention. Let me get you home."

Overhearing the conversation, the medical personnel say it's their job to transport him to a hospital. Bertha objects but the police stepped in. She has no choice but to back off. Breeze is loaded into the medical van and rushed away. Bertha is able to hale down a taxi and goes straight to the hospital.

Sitting in the hospital's waiting room, Bertha is being confronted by a Doctor. "He's going to be okay. Just a flush wound. Nothing to worry about. However, we will have to keep him overnight for observation."

Bertha is home alone in her apartment, partly undressed, still feeling the hurt from her own pain plus what has happened to Breeze. she climbs into bed crying and lay until falling into sleep.

Three days later, Breeze is released from the hospital and back at home. Bertha is upset and has not been able to sleep thinking about what has happened to Breeze that put him in the hospital. Still upset, at night, she cried loud enough to wake Breeze.

Feeling slightly better himself, Breeze goes to Bertha's room. 'KNOCK. KNOCK.' He would walk in yawning and calling out to her. "MOM."

Bertha would see him from her bed. "Sorry. I didn't mean to wake you."

"No problem. I heard noises coming from your room and just wanted to see if you were okay."

"I am baby."

He would sometime get into her bed and allow her to hug him from behind while she sobs and stroked his hair.

"Mom, it's going to be okay." He would often say. "We'll get through this. I'll be back to work in no time and you'll get better under the doctor's care." She smiled. "Don't worry about me. I'll be fine. It's you I'm worried about."

Several day later, Trashman and 6 of his gang member pull a raid on Miller Homes. They go through tenants in the courtyard at gun point taking their money and other items of value. Word has gotten out to the police department about the robbery. They go out to investigate. Tenants are in fear of retaliation and refuse to give any information to the police. They leave puzzled and without any information.

A week goes by, Breeze goes to Candyman's apartment. Candyman is home alone watching television. There are several knocks on the door. He goes to open it. It's Breeze. Candyman is not looking to cool at Breeze. "Come on in," he says. "I want you to run down to me just what happened that get you shot."

"Like I said, I didn't do anything. Those two hanging around that med store knew I worked for you. So, they thought I was working in their area and they wanted me out. The first time I went to the med store, they told me if I came back, they would do something to me. This is the only place I know that sells the type of meds my mom needs. So I have to go there. Just before he shot me, I was told by the tall skinny one he was only going to hurt me this time. But if they sees me around there again, I'll be killed. Period. Point blank."

Candyman showed signs of anger. I'm gonna take care of this. You can start back on your route tomorrow. Cool?"

"Thanks. I'll be here."

"Stay away from that med store for the next couple of days. Or go late at night just before closing only if you really need to go."

Breeze says in a shy way. "My mom's meds are getting low. I need some cash."

Candyman reaches into his pocket and pulls out a wad of money. "No problem. How much do you need? Anything to help your mom. You still going to that other gig?"

"No. I quit that to spend more time working for you. I'll pay you back after I start working again and that should be next week."

"Take care of your mom first. Pay me after you get straight. How much do you need?"

"Five hundred should get me over."

The next evening Candyman, Bill and Buck drive to the med store. They see two gang members standing outside near the doorway talking and laughing. Candyman drives up close to where the two are. Bill and Buck are sitting on the passenger's side. They let down their window. The two members see what is happening and start to run. Bill and Buck open fire, dropping both to the concrete pavement. The car speeds away and out of sight.

Upon returning to Miller Homes, those who knew Bertha as a good spoke's person asked her if she would come back to head up the meetings with town officials in their fight to make Miller Homes suitable for living. She accepted because she had a lot on her mine, especially having to deal with poor living conditions that never seemed to be addressed and the violence that never seem to end.

The meetings were being held at City Hall on the lower level. Bertha arrived with eyes swollen from crying. She wore her hair curled up and dressed in decent clothing. A blouse and a pair of well pressed slacks. As usual, the room was filled with ELDERS from Miller Homes chattering. She went to stand in the back of the crowd near a wall. She looked around the room and spotted a familiar face. Flash's Aunt was sitting with her back facing Bertha and talking to a person seated next to her.

The mayor, a light brown skin man wearing a dark business suit walked into the room followed by two officers. The three walked to the front of the crowd. The mayor stepped to the front of the crowd by way of a small platform. The two officers retreated to a wall directly behind him keeping a straight face and watching for any potential trouble makers. The mayor opened the meeting my saying, "Good evening ladies and gentlemen of Miller Homes." He put on a big smile. The people settled down and the chatter in the room died.

"What I have to say may not be pleasing to all of you. We all know Miller Homes is a hard nut to crack when it comes to ridding crime from that area. With our limited police force and little or no cooperation from tenants, our hands are tied as to how to handle your problems.

May I be so kind as to ask for a few suggestions from any of you who wish to speak?"

An older man clutching a cane struggles as he comes to his feet. "What happened to the officers that were patrolling Miller Homes? I felt safe when they were around."

"They have been reassigned due to injuries they received from there."

"I think they were punks if they let those youngsters beat up on them." The crowd broke out into laughter.

The mayor held his hand high above his head to silence them. He asked. "Is there another?"

An elder lady takes her stand. "Mr. Mayor. It's hard walking up to the seventh floor at my age. Every time I leave my apartment, there are guys hanging around in my hallway. They keep leaving trash all over the hallway. When I return, they are still there making the hallway smell bad with the stuff they are smoking. The worst part is they are asking me for money. I'm on a fixed income and I can't afford to support their habit. They tell me if I don't give them money, they might hurt me. I can live like this. What can you do about it?"

He signals for the two police officers to come to him. He whispers something to them and they return to the back wall. The lady is still standing. "See me after the meeting. Is there another?" She takes her seat.

Bertha moved from the wall and walks into the center isle. "Mr. Mayor. Maintenance has been pretty bad at miller Homes. You just heard how dirty the hallways are. People living on the upper floors have been walking up those steps for years. I know if you lived there, those elevators would have been fixed the very next day." The crowd rose up in a loud, quick agreement. "Do the older folk a favor and stop having them do force marches up and down those steps. And while you're at it, hose down those hallways. Sooner rather than later, somebody is going to pass out from the bad smells. If you were on our side Mr. Mayor, you would have been over there to see the condition our people are living in. Try living like us for once. I know I'm talking to the wall." The crowd agreed. "Also, crime has gotten really bad on the courtyard. Kids are playing out there and who knows what danger they are facing. You could make Miller Homes safer by placing someone at those doors entrance to keep the riff raff out. I think this would make most of the tenants feel safer." Bertha turned and as she is walking away from the meeting with tears in her eyes. The old man called out to her. "You go girl. You set him straight." The people in the room started chattering among themselves in agreement.

Outside the room, Bertha stopped to breathe. She held her stomach as she slightly groaned in pain. People passing her in the hallway only looked at her and no one stopped to offer help. After waiting for a few minutes, she started feeling better and continued to walk toward home.

Outside the building, the darkness of night has set in and the eerie of silence surrounded her. She stopped and stifled a cry while holding her bag tightly toward her.

Mark, who just happened to be on the street watching Linda and Dee Dee trying to catch a trick happened to see Bertha coming down the opposite side of the street. He called out to her from a shadowed area. "Hey Bertha!"

Bertha jumped at the sound of the voice and sees the faint shadow of a standing body by one of the trees. Because of the pain eating away at her and the darkness, she doesn't recognize who is there or the voice. She continued walking. Mark crosses the street and quickly catches up to be beside her. "Hey Bertha, remember me. Mark?"

Bertha puts on a straight face trying to hide the pain. She wipes away tears from her face.

"What's with you?" He ask.

"I got this pain in my stomach and I'm feeling really, really bad."

"Sorry to hear that. It's the cancer isn't it?"

"Yeah. I think so."

The pain is causing her to walk slower. Mark keeps pace with her while smoking a cigarette.

Street lights shine on their face. Bertha tenses down. Mark wraps his arm around her shoulder. Bertha started crying. Mark starts to feel her pain. "Don't cry baby. I know what you need." He hands her the marijuana cigarette he has been smoking. She takes a puff and immediately starts coughing.

"Feel better?"

Bertha closes her eyes while her head is starting to feel heavy. She nods and starts drifting toward the street. Mark pulls her back. "Come on. Let's get you home."

CHAPTER Four

Sunshine is peeking through the curtains. The sound of traffic and the light twittering comes in from outside. Mark's light snores fill the room. The bedroom door is ajar. Breeze walks in. Mark is laying in his mom's bed.

Breeze is startled. He calls out. "Mom"?

Bertha opens her eyes and groan.

Breeze calls again louder. "MOM?"

She responds not fully awake, "Breeze." She moved to a position where she can sit up with her back against the bed frame while massaging her head and holding up a blanket against her partly naked body. Mark shifts beside her still sleeping.

Breeze stares at her. "Aren't you supposed to be at work?"

"What time is it?" She looks at her bed side table digital clock. Clock is reading 3:04 pm. "Oh. No." She calls out.

Breeze shakes his head in disappointment and exits the room.

"Breeze wait!" She calls out. A few second later, she hears him slamming the front door shut. Bertha jumps, closes her eyes and exhales sharply.

Mark stirs in the bed and slowly shows signs of waking up. His eyes become fully open as he looks toward Bertha. "What was that I heard?"

"It was my kid."

"Did he have to make that much noise closing that door?"

Bertha looks at him with anger in her eyes. "Yeah, and you need to leave." She gets up from the bed and throws cover over Mark's face. He removes it. Moving away from the bed, she grabs a shirt from the floor and gets dressed.

Mark looks at her confused. "Are you mad at me, baby?"

She picks up Mark's shirt and pants and throws them at him. "Just leave."

Mark puts on his clothes. He becomes angry. "Fine. But I'll be back." He exits the room and slams the front door shut. Bertha flinches at the sound. "If they don't soon fix that door, I'm gonna tear it off. It's starting to drive me half crazy every time that happens." She walks to the right side of the night stand beside the bed. Picks up her medication bottle, stares at the prescribed dosage and returns it to the stand.

Breeze goes back to work doing his usual route of collecting money in exchange for papers. Today has been a bad day for him. In Tower Two, one of the customers on the list was handed a newspaper. He told Breeze to wait while he closed the door and goes to get the payment. Breeze waits five minutes. He knocks again. Still no one comes. He leaves without receiving money owed. On top of that, he has had a hard night and didn't get much sleep. A tired look draped his face as he counts out the money and hands it to Candyman. Candyman stares at him. "You're short." Breeze takes out his list. He points to an apartment on the sheet. "The man right here." (pointing at the address} "Took the paper and never gave me the doe. I waited, but he never returned."

"I'll take care of this." He hands Breeze his cut of the cash. Breeze gives back two-hundred as part of the payment on his loan. Candyman goes to the man's apartment. When he opens the door, Candyman starts beating on him.

The man starts shouting. "Sorry. I didn't mean to do it."

"You owe me. Pay up." The man goes off and returns with the doe." Next time you short me, I'm gonna shorten your life. Do you hear me? Or do I need to repeat myself? If I do, you ain't gonna like what comes next."

The man has blood coming from his nose and mouth. "I hear you. It won't happens again."

Breeze is sitting on the only functional swing on the courtyard smoking a cigarette looking upset. Two black police officers walk toward him. The light skin one walks straight up to him. The other brown skin officer stands back a couple of feet. "Hey kid. You from around here?"

"I'm not a kid. And why you asking me?"

"Can we talk?"

"About what?"

The brown skin one looks at Breeze a little annoyed with him starting his game of 20 questions. He confronts Breeze. "What's with this game you're playing?"

Breeze brushes him off.

The other light skin one turns back to Breeze. "We just want to ask you some questions about the people living around here."

"I don't know anything and I don't know these people. You got the wrong person."

The cop standing back becomes angary. "Listen kid."

Breeze shoots back. "Stop calling me a kid."

"Whatever. You're not in any trouble. We just need to ask you a few questions about the shootings."

Breeze doesn't make eye contact. He takes a long drag from his cigarette, holds it in for a couple of seconds and releases it.

The cops are not leaving and Breeze is starting to tense up. The light skin cop is starting to apply pressure on him. "What do you know about those two men killed near the drug store? And did you know them?"

"No. Not really. I wasn't there when it happened. So, stop pumping me for answers."

The brown skin cop standing back stares at Breeze. "Say. Aren't you the kid who got shot by the drug store?"

"You got the wrong person. You need to go looking for that kid. When you find him, you just might get your answers from him."

"You sure look like him."

"How old are you anyway? You seem too young to be smoking."

"That's none of your business."

Both cops look at each other disappointed. Breeze looked unimpressed as he flicked the last of his cigarette to the ground and mashes it with his shoe.

The brown skin cop speaks low to his partner. "Why are we wasting time interrogating this kid?"

Breeze lifts his head, but doesn't say a word.

The other cop grunts in agreement. He shifts his attention back to Breeze while putting his hands on his knees so he can be at eye level with him. "Look. I know you think this doesn't concern you, but if you see anything at all, don't hesitate to call us."

Breeze stands. "Officers, don't be bothering me. I need to be somewhere else right now. I got'ta bounce. See ya." He started walking away.

"We only trying to help." Called out the light skin cop.

Breeze turns his head toward them speaking sarcastic. "Yeah. I'll let you know."

Breeze goes to Candyman's apartment. The two are sitting on the couch. Breeze tells him about the cops. "The cops been hanging around the Homes every since them two dude got wasted."

Candyman picks up a cigarette from an end table. He holds it out in front of Breeze. "What are they asking?"

"A bunch of nothing. Just trying to pump some scoop out of people on how and who iced them."

Candyman lights a cigarette, takes a puff and places it in an ashtray. "Trashman should take better care of his people. What a shame."

"Yeah. Glad they're out of the way. No problem now getting mom's meds."

"You doing good out there. Just keep your nose clean."

"Mom thinks I'm doing good on my job. Mark got her believing I got a raise."

"When you joined in on the paper route, you made a smart move. You can see how its paying off. It was a raise."

The two police officers have been walking around the Miller Homes buildings part of the day. They see Trashman and members of his gang coming through the parking lot. The gang split up in search for victims to rob. The gang is bold. Two member walk up to a car and stick a gun into the driver's face and demand money. The two police officers see what is going down and rush to the scene. Before the gang members can rob the driver, the police officers close in on them. Another gang member show up and force the two police officers to drop their guns. Trashman comes over and picks up the guns from the ground. Looks them over. "Nice pieces. I think I'll keep them for myself."

The light skin police officer tell Trashman. "You ain't gonna get away with this."

"You piece of crap. I just did."

The two gang members force the drive and passengers to hand over their wallets. The gang runs off.

The two police officers reported to the Chief's office. They tell him about their bad ordeal at Miller Homes. He sits and thinks for a moment. "Here's my idea. I'm going to reassign both of you to another area. In return, I'm going to send 4 plain officers there so we can catch the crooks. Do you know the gang member who took both of your guns?"

"Yeah." Said the light skin one while the other shook his head in agreement.

"I'm gonna sent you over there to point them out."

Breeze arrived at Bertha's apartment. Mark is cooking dinner. Breeze is not at all pleased with him. "You and your bright ideas." Breeze said in an angary tone of voice. "Me making this doe to help my mom, got me shot and two other dudes killed. Now the cops are asking me questions and I'm one of the victims. That really sucks."

Mark turned from the stove. "You ain't got nothing to worry about. Did you tell them anything?"

"Remember, I'm just a dumb paper boy working a route."

"Don't look at it that way. Just think. If you wasn't doing the route, your mom might really be doing bad without the meds you buying for her."

Breeze had to think for a moment. He began to calm down. "Yeah. I guess you're right."

Bertha walks into the apartment. "Smells good," she says as she makes her way to the bath room.

Mark speaks in a low voice. "Don't quit the route. Remember your mom."

Bertha returns. "Is dinner ready?"

Candyman is pacing the floor in his apartment while Bill and Buck are sitting on the couch watching him. "Those cops look like they're gonna be trouble," he says.

"I don't think so," says Buck. "I didn't see anybody around when the deal went down."

"Good. I hope so. Don't nobody know about this except us and maybe the paper boy. I ain't finished talking with him."

After dinner, Mark, Bertha and Breeze continue to sit at the table. Mark stands. "I gotta be going. Business waiting."

"Thanks for cooking dinner. After working all day and dealing with this pain, I sort of lost it when it comes to doing things around this apartment."

"Don't worry baby. I got your back."

Breeze gives him a dirty look as he looks up from the table, but doesn't say a word.

Mark makes his way to the door. Bertha returns to the table and sits across from Breeze.

Breeze gives his mom the same dirty look. "He got your back all right."

"Don't say it like that. Why you so angary at him?"

"Mom. He don't work. He's a hustler. He's got girls working for him on the street and he's always cheating people out of their money." Breeze has her thinking. "I keep telling you he's no good. Also, he don't give respect to anybody. You stay with him long enough and you will see. I keep telling you, I'm done with him."

Bertha reaches across the table, picks up a jar of pills and downs two while placing the jar back on the table.

Breeze hands her a glass of water. She drinks a little at a time.

Bertha sees him raise his fist and bangs it on the table in anger. "I don't like him around here. He needs to go."

She is not moved by his action. "I can't see why you don't like him. Maybe you two will grow on each other. He's a sweet guy. Plus he helps around here." She picks up a small bottle and shakes it a couple of times. There is no sound inside. Carefully she reads the instructions and returned it to the table.

Breeze looks at her seriously. "You're not listening to me." He talks softly. "I can take care of you."

"I'm listening. Baby, I know you can."

"He's using you."

"You know it's not like that."

"And you're using him."

Bertha tries to speak.

Breeze stops her. "I can't believe you." Slightly angered, he stands and walks toward the door.

Bertha's eyes follow him. "Baby, can you get me more medication?"

"Sure mom." He walked back and she handed him a bottle and holds his hand. "Don't be so mean."

"If he got your back, why didn't he ask you if you needed anything?"

"You know he was just trying to be nice."

"Nice my foot." Breeze takes the bottle and heads toward the door. She puts her finger into her ears as he opens it and slams it shut.

The 4 plain clothes officers arrive at Miller Homes. They are friendly toward the tenants. The light skin police officer shows up. The tenants are not as friendly toward outside strangers in their area. The officers spend most of the day observing things in and around the area. Things seemed to be normal and quiet. None of Trashman's gang nor Trashman himself showed up. All the officers leave for the day.

At the drug store, Breeze orders her meds. The cashier brings the order up front and laid it on the counter. She rings up a tab. The order comes $250. He has to leave it because he only has $200. He heads back toward Bertha's apartment. The street is empty. He walks with both hands in his pockets wondering where can he get the extra money. His thoughts go to asking Candyman for another small loan. Suddenly, he spots a lone lady walking in the distance. She has a purse partly hanging from her shoulder. He looks around and notice no one is present in the area. "BINGO!"

He runs up behind her and swipes the purse. In shock, the lady starts yelling at the top on her lungs. "THIEF. SOMEBODY HELP ME!" Breeze runs as fast as he can. She starts running after him but stops because of her older age. Plus he is too fast for her. He turns a corner and loses her. He sees and alley and runs down inside to hide behind a dumpster sweating and breathing heavily. He opens the bag and looks for the wallet. Not able to find it, he grabs the items and throws the contents onto the concrete. The contents make soft thumping sounds as the lipstick, power case and other items bounce around near his feet. Still, no wallet. He shakes the bag upside down and a small money case falls out. He picks it up and opens it only to find four twenties, one ten and one five dollar bill inside. He becomes frustrated whispering to himself. "That's all." He throws the case and bag onto the concrete and kicks the bag violently. Suddenly, he hears the sound of a police siren coming from a far distance coming in his direction. He began to panic and ducks down on the far side of the dumpster. The car pulled up near the alley. He can hear two people speaking in a low voice. A light begins shining down through the alley reflecting above the walls. The light passes over where he is hiding. He waits for a few minutes hoping the coast is clear and gets up, climbs onto the dumpster and jumped over the wall beside it. He runs as fast as he can hoping to lose them.

The next day, the 4 police officer return to Miller Homes without the light skin officer. One goes into Tower One. Another goes into Tower Two. The third one goes into the parking lot and the last one stays in the courtyard. About an hour later, 5 of Trashman's gang members show up in the parking lot. They go to stand around a car with the engine running. The police officer in the parking lot suspect something funny is going on and calls his other 3 officers to the parking lot. Just as the gang pull the driver from his vehicle, all 4 officers place the 5 under arrest. Later that evening the 5 are brought before the judge. The man who was attacked in the Miller Homes parking lot refused to press charges and the 5 are released. One of the police officers reports back to the chief with the bad news. The police chief listens and becomes furious. "Them darn people over there want us to clean up the place, but refuse to support us. Maybe we should be locking them up."

Mark's apartment is filled with clothing items laying everywhere. Linda refuses to clean up after him. He is not happy with her. She's been sitting on a bean bag smoking something through a glass pipe. The music is playing and she is trying to sing through her intoxicated state. Mark sits on the couch watching her as she tries to stand but falls backward. She rolls over on her side and is able to push herself to her knees and onto her feet and starts dancing.

Mark looks away. "See what I have to go through?" Just plain talking out loud. Linda hears him.

"You saying something about me?"

"Yeah. I hope you heard what I said."

"You need to keep your mouth shut. Half the time, you don't make any sense."

"Chill with that. How much money did you make last night?" She stops dancing and reaches into her pocket, pull out a wad of bills. Hands it to him. He counts them and give her a small piece while he lays the remain bills on a coffee table in front of him. "Keep it up. You doing good." She goes back to dancing.

There's a faint knock at the door. "Linda!" He calls out. She doesn't respond. He calls again louder. "LINDA!" She stops dancing and looks at him. "Get that. Somebody's at the door." She goes to opens it and becomes face to face with Trashman. He pushes his way past her as he enters the apartment. Mark sees him and jumps straight up from his seat slightly in shock.

Trashman walks up to him and stands toe to toe with him. He removes his sun glasses and gives him a mean look. "You ran off the other day without giving me all my doe. I came to collect. Now hand it over." He holds out his hand.

Mark is feeling uneasy. He has his hands in his pockets. "I left because you and Candyman had something going on and I didn't want to get caught up in it."

"I said give me my doe. I don't want hear it."

Mark looks down at the money he just received from Linda. He picks it up from the table. "Here." He hands the money over. Trashman counts it. "You short. Where's the rest?"

"I'm working on it."

Trashman turned mean. "Don't work on it. Get it. The next time we meet. If you don't have it, you better pray I don't have you covered with growing flowers. You get my drift. I don't play when it comes to people owing me."

"Money is hard to come…."

He grabs Mark by his shirt and twist it. "What did I say? I don't want'ta hear it." He pushes Mark backwards onto his couch. Turns and walks out through the still partly opened door.

Linda looks at Mark. "See. You keep giving me a hard time. He's gonna kick your butt and I'm gonna laugh when he does it."

"Shut up," he says in anger.

"No. Now you see how I feel with you messing with me. Scared hah?"

"I said SHUT UP! You talk too much."

Linda goes toward her room singing. "That butt's gonna shine and it ain't gonna be mine if you don't get that money to him in time."

The next morning, Sally goes into her kitchen. She sees spots of water near her kitchen sink. See goes up close to see what might the problem be. As she bends over to investigate the possible problem, she sees a fine drip of water leaking from one of the pipes. She goes to the phone and calls the main office. In the meantime, a group of drug dealers are operating in and around her building. A white maintenance service technician person has been contacted to check on the problem. As he enters the building the drug dealers give him the eye. He pay very little attention to them as he makes his way to Sally's apartment. While in Sally's apartment two police officers come up to the same floor and go to the apartment across from hers. They enter the apartment by kicking in the door. Later, they come out, carrying a young, black male in hand cuff. Sally goes to her door after hearing all the noise to investigate. She see the black male being taken down the hallway and down the steps and out of the building. Later, the maintenance service man finishes the job and leaves Sally's apartment. Upon exiting the building, the drug dealers see the man and approach him. One of the dealers approaches him. "We saw you go into the building and we saw the cops taking one of our boys away. We believe you to be a cop."

The man was quick to defend himself. "OH. You got this all wrong. I was just doing a called in job."

"You lying to us. We saw the cops with the dude."

The man went into panic. "I had nothing to do with that."

One of the dealers raised a fist to his face. "If we see you around here again, you ain't gonna be leaving out of here happy. You got that?"

The man left and never returned.

CHAPTER Five

Bertha goes to visit Sally after work. Sally has just finished cooking and is getting ready to fix herself a plate when there's a knock on the door. Bertha knocks again and suddenly the door opens. A sudden shock of pain causes Bertha to slightly bend forward. Sally takes notice and shows concern. "What's happening Bertha?"

Bertha doesn't make immediate comment about her condition. She can barely speak. "My whole world seems to be falling apart."

"How so? Come on in."

Bertha walks in still bending slightly over with one hand pressing against her stomach. "What happened to the door across from you?"

Sally was quick to say. "The cops did it. They got one of those drug dealers out of here."

"It's about time. They are a mess. Did you know Breeze was shot several weeks ago."

Sally places her hand close to her mouth. "Oh my GOD. No, I didn't know." She looks at Bertha partly in shock.

"Not bad. He's doing okay now and is back to work."

"Thank God it wasn't serious."

What did they say was the cause?" "Yeah. I was thanking God also. Then I was feeling sick on the job and my whole world instantly disappeared on me as I passed out. They called 911 and I ended up in the hospital for several days. The Doctor tells me I was lucky I had friends around me when it happened. All I know is that when I can too, she was standing by my side. "Bertha, can you hear me." And those were the first few words I heard."

"I hope it wasn't serious."

Bertha looks down at the floor than back at her. "The Doctor said it is cancer."

Sally gasped. "Oh my Lord!" Almost going into shock for a few seconds. she calmed down believing she was scaring Bertha. "Girl, you can get through this. You need to pray and stay on your doctor plus get some treatments. Let's go have a seat." They go into the front room and sit next to each other.

"I know Breeze is making good money on his job and is helping me with most of the money situations I need to handle my medications and other needs."

"You have a great son. Thank God for him."

"Yeah. Thank God. And then there's my friend Mark. He helps with cooking and other things around the apartment. He is really a great guy."

"Sounds like you have plenty of help. Care for a plate of food? I just finished cooking."

"Smells good. What did you cook?"

"Oh, some chicken."

Bertha began to laugh. "Before I go. I want to tell you a little story about something our family had when I was a little girl."

"Sure. I would love to hear some more of your stories from years long ago."

"You wouldn't believe this. We had the strangest pet."

"What was that?"

"Well after the fire in the basement, we got two dogs and later when we made our yearly trip down south, my grandmother was given a baby chick from her sister who had chickens running wild just about everywhere all over the place."

"You had a fire?"

"Yeah. But that's another story."

"What kind of a pet is a chicken?"

"I don't know. Anyway, we brought this baby chick back with us. All my aunts and uncles got to liking this chick and started treating it as if it was one of the family. The chick grew up to be a pretty good size chicken. One day there must have been a shortage of food in the home. So, while everyone was away except grandmother, she killed the chicken and had it ready for supper."

"That's sad. Who would eat a pet?"

"I guess back in those days, money was hard to come by. People needed food. Especially for large families. My grandparents had eight kid living at home with me making nine. When it was time for everyone to eat, as custom, someone would always go out back and feed the chicken around the time everyone came to the table. It was funny that no one ever served themselves until everyone was seated. Anyway, my grandmother uncovered this golden brown chicken in the center of the table. One of my aunts who had gone out to feed the chicken asked when she returned, where was the chicken that was usually kept in the back yard. Everyone looked at each other without saying a word. They looked at the fried chicken and all left the table. My grandmother decided to give the parts she and grandfather didn't want to the dogs. They sniff at the parts and walked away just like the family did."

"I guess your grandmother knew what she was doing to feed the family. That was a large family. I know my parents believed in having a lot of kids that would help support them in their older age years. Times have changed since then. With the cost of everything these days, one can just barely provide for themselves. So, what did you eat? My mom fixed me a plate of vegetables."

"I guess by you bring a child, you didn't have any choice."

"I guess you're right. No thanks for the food. Just stopping by. Haven't seen you in a while since we talked the last time. I want to keep in contact with friends. You know how some people are."

"Always glad to see you."

"Like by son says, 'Got'ta Bounce."

Sally looked puzzled. "Got'ta who?"

Bertha laughs. "Got'ta bounce is slang for got'ta be leaving."

Sally started laughing as well. "Kids these days say the funniest things."

"Tell me about it. I'll see you again when things get a little better with me."

They stood from the couch and Sally led Bertha to the door. When Sally opened it, Bertha walked out. They both waved good-bye as a jester and Bertha walked to the end of the hallway and disappeared.

Candyman became good friends with Flash's Aunt after flash was placed behind bars. Every now and then, Candyman would drop-bye and give her a hand with whatever she needed. Night had fallen and Candyman was going to visit Auntie. He was dressed in a dark hooded sweater as he knocked on Auntie's door repetitively. No answer. He knew Auntie claimed she had a hearing problem and sometimes it took her a while to realize sounds were being made around her. He stopped knocking because his knuckles were getting sore. As he stood waiting for the door to open, he could hear Breeze and Buck's voices in a distance coming up the stairway. He started banging again with an open hand so he could hurry inside, trying to avoid them. Through the pounding, he was able to make out their conversation.

Buck tells Breeze, "I'm just saying Candyman ain't fair with our cut."

Breeze stops to think. He looks a little worried. "I don't know man. I don't wanna get on his bad side."

Candyman shifts his attention toward the two coming in his direction but still out in sight. He touches the gun tucked in the holder under his hooded sweater thinking they might try something. He couldn't help it but to start talking to himself. "If they feel they should be getting more money for the chances and risk they're taking, maybe I should get a new bunch of dudes or just hat up to a new location." He continued banging on the door non-stop. "She said she'd be home." Suddenly, she opens the door and is surprised to see him. He rushes in passing her before she could say a word in a paranoid state of mind. He calls back to her, "Close the door. They can't know I'm here."

Auntie looked confused. She stuck her head out into the hallway. It's empty. She ducks back in, closing the door and walks straight up to Candyman. "Who?" She asked.

"It's none of your business."

"You must have been hanging around with Flash much too long. You starting to think and act just like him."

Candyman started to relax now that he felt secure. Auntie reaches out and gave him a tight hug. Then goes off toward the kitchen. "What's wrong dear? You hungry? I made dinner."

Candyman starts holding his stomach. "Yeah, starving." Candyman and Auntie sit at the table. On the table is placed, roast beef, buttered corn, string beans, mash potatoes, and gravy and a large bottle of cranberry juice. Candyman dumps a heap of potatoes and roast beet onto his plate and pours gravy over them.

She looks at his body. "How have you been? Looks like you losing weight. You're starting to look as thin as a lamp post."

"Same. Nothing much changed. You okay here Auntie? Anybody giving you troubles?" He shoves a spoonful of potatoes into his mouth. Gravy sticks to his lips and sucks the potatoes in while smacking his lips in delight. "This is really good stuff."

"Thank you. Everything's fine except those steps could be a pain in my legs sometimes."

"I got room at my crib. You could hang out over there. I could be your runner up and down the steps."

She holds her hands up. "No. No. I couldn't possibly leave this place. There are far too many memories." She brings them down to rest on the table. Then started looking around at the small area of her small apartment with a melancholic look on her face. She sees a picture of a young man resembling Flash with dark features which she claimed to be her late husband.

Candyman interrupted her thoughts while loading his mouth. "This place is a dump, Auntie."

"I wouldn't call it that. I've been fine here for all these years I've been here. And I'll be fine until the day I leave here."

Candyman pushes more food into his mouth. His words come out all garbled. "I don't know why you think this place is safe. Anyway. Where you going?"

"Didn't your mama ever tell you not to talk with food in your mouth?"

"Yeah. I know. But she would do it and ask me questions at the same time. She would get mad if I didn't answer her, so I was only doing what she was doing."

"Poor example." She pours him a glassful of cranberry juice. He chugged down the juice as fast as a person would be pouring water down a drain. She could only look at him in amazement. "When was the last time you ate?"

"Early this morning."

"I'll be leaving here when the LORD calls. The mayor said he'll be providing extra security for Miller Homes, especially for us old folks in the meantime."

"The mayor, huh. Listening to him is like fishing in a pond with no fish in it." He takes another spoonful to his mouth.

She looks at him in amazement as dumps one spoon of food after another into his mouth. "Especially since several folks been killed in that lot in the past several years. And some of the younger people were killed right in front of this building. Can you believe that?"

Candyman slightly chokes on his food. He immediately pours himself another glass of juice and chugged it down like he did the other and slammed the glass on the table.

Auntie flinched. "Careful. Don't go breaking up my glasses."

"Which is exactly why you should be moving away from here."

"The only way I'll leave here is that they put me out. And I can't see that."

"I just want you to be safe. Can you dig it?" They ate in silence under the sound of clinking utensils and plates. After dinner, he went into Flash's bedroom.

Looked at a few things. Picked up several items and returned them. Then laid on the bed and fell asleep.

    Bertha sat at home smoking marijuana through a small pipe by the kitchen window. She draws the curtains leaving only a small space for her to see through. Her eyes are trained on watching people coming and going. Her vision is drawn away by a car moving along slowly on the parking lot. Suddenly there are BEEP, BEEP, BEEPs coming from her cell phone where it sits on a coffee table. She goes to see who the call is coming from. By the time she reaches it, the ID shows a missed call. She could tell it was from Monique by looking at the numbers. She is in no mood to speak with her so she walks away from the phone.

    Mark comes into the apartment looking high on uppers. He sways a little as he made his way to Bertha and manages to kiss her on her neck without falling. Bertha doesn't like his condition and tried to push him away. He manages to grab her arm to study himself. "You look a mess," she said eyeing him up and down. He lets her arm go and start aggressively unbuttoning her blouse to a point where it is almost off. This is making her angary. "Mark! Stop! I'm not in the mood."

    He doesn't listen. He takes off his belt.

    She pushes at him in an attempt to distance herself. "I said quit."

Mark comes back close to her and pulls on her hair while trying to kiss her on the neck. "You like that?"

"No. WOO. You're hurting me." She twist and turn her head. "LET GO!"

Breeze comes into the apartment. He instantly sees Mark man handling his mother and runs to punch him in the back of his head. Mark, not feeling much pain, let go of her hair to feel the spot where he was just hit by Breeze. He turn around to face him.

"So you wan'na fight me with those bee stingers of yours?"

Breeze is blazing mad. "I told you not to be hurting my mom. Now you gonna see the other side of me."

"Am I suppose to take that as a threat? I'm gon'na kick your little skinny butt." Mark raises both fist but because he is impaired, he starts swaying as he drift sideways in his approach toward Breeze.

Breeze takes advantage of Mark being off balance and is able to throw two stiff shots into Mark's face. Mark falls backward onto the floor. Breeze advanced to stand over him. He looks down at Mark who places one hand over a spot where Breeze had landed the last solid punch.

Breeze screams at him. "Get up punk. I ain't finished with you yet."

Bertha grabs Breeze by the arm. "Breeze honey, stop before somebody gets hurt. Oh my GOD. What am I going to do now?" She pulls on Breeze arm. He tries to shake her loose. She screams. "STOP!"

Breeze steps back. Bertha releases his arm. Still mad and full of anger, "Mom, I can't let him do this to you. I tried telling you he's bad news. Please listen to me."

"Let me deal with this." She says partly between being in shock and panicky.

Mark raises a fist toward Breeze. "You got that one off. You better watch your back because I'm gonna be on it."

Breeze stomps on Mark's chest while he is trying to lift himself from the floor but is pushed back.

Bertha grabs Breeze's arm again. "He's just having a bad moment."

Breeze raises his fist and points it at Mark. "See this. I got your bad moment." Then he turned to his mom and shakes it to show he means business.

"Honey, please stop." She is starting to sob. "Things are going to be okay. Why don't you go for a walk or go to your room until you cool off."

"How can I cool off with this piece of trash doing this to you?"

"Breeze, Please."

"Okay mom. I'm gonna go for a walk, but when I come back and see any burses on you, he's gonna be a dead man." He looks down at Mark and removed his foot from Mark's chest. "You better be glad my mom stopped me. Next time she won't be able to help you." He kicks Mark hard on the side of his ribs. Mark makes a sorry out cry. Breeze walks out the door talking to himself. Mark lays groaning from his pains. "He's gonna pay for this. Yeah. Highly."

"Keep talking like that and you won't be coming here anymore."

Breeze's father was a hard working man. He lived not far from Miller Homes. Breeze had not visited him during the time he and Bertha had been back. He would go to see him and ask if he could camp out there until things settled at home. He knew they were on good standings from the last time he saw him. That was over 5 years ago. He, at that time was living alone. Breeze walked up to the door. Knocked. A young lady came to the door. Breeze looked at her in a surprising way. He didn't expect to see a lady.

"Can I help you?" She asked.

Breeze kindly asked, "is my father home?"

The lady looked surprisingly at him. "Your father? I'm sorry but I live here alone."

"How so? Do you know where he went?"

"No. He moved away from here a few years ago. I last spoke to him at the time he was selling this house. He said he was moving away because there was nothing left here for him. His lady friend with the kid had already left I assume that's you. So, he packed up and was gone. No telling where he might be now."

Breeze stepped back from the door. "Sorry to have bothered you. Have a nice day." Now Breeze was going to Candyman's apartment.

Candyman, Bill and Buck are sitting around putting newspapers together. As Breeze knocked on the door, Bill stops to lets Breeze enter the apartment. He goes back to helping. Breeze walks up to Candyman and watches for a few minutes. "Say Candyman, can I camp out here for a couple of days?"

Candyman looks up toward Breeze. "Yeah. What brought this on?"

"I don't know. Things ain't right at the crib. Mark's treating mom bad, and me and him got into a fight. Mom's taking his side and this thing is all messed up."

"I don't see any burses on you. Did you do a job on him?"

Breeze smiles. "Yeah. I broke his face and maybe cracked a rib or two. That's when mom thought I was going to put his lights out for good." They all started laughing.

"You need help? We can finish him off for you."

"No. Mom's gonna figure out I had something to do with it and things might not be going in my favor. She's already down on me for putting the bad mouth on him."

"Sound like you really did a job on him. Take the spear bedroom on the right."

"Thanks. I owe you."

"No you don't. We good. Just keep doing the route."

Buck points to Breeze. "Don't let this problem got the best of you. You know we're here for you."

"Maybe somewhere down the line, I might be calling on you guys."

Mark continues feeling a slight pain from the kick. He manages to get on his feet and make his way to the coffee table where he draws three lines of cocaine. He slowly bent down while holding his side and bending on one knee to snort up two lines.

Bertha looks at him with fear in her eyes. "I'd rather you don't do that here."

He shoots back. "I'll do whatever I want. And as for that punk son of yours, you need to talk to him or there's gon'na be plenty of trouble around here. I ain't gon'na forget this happened."

"You don't have to keep warning me. If things get any worse, you got to go."

Bertha's imagination started to run wild within her. She looks down. Sees Marcus, pale ghostly figure looking directly from the front of the building. She doesn't move. Mark continues to snort cocaine in the background. Marcus' figure disappears.

Water is rushing from the shower. Bertha, with blood-shot eyes stands in front of the sink and mirror wrapped in a towel. The sound of the shower's water drowns out the sound of her weeping sob. She pulls at her hair looking distraught and crazy like. She reaches in and turns off the shower and goes back to taking a closer look at herself in the mirror. She sees dark circles under her eyes. She reaches up to touch her face and wipes away both streams of tears.

Candyman is walking out of the main entrance of Tower One. He see Bill and Buck standing near a bench. He goes to be with them. They start talking and to Candyman's surprise, he sees Trashman wearing shorts, a hat and sunglasses walking across the Tower grounds while talking and walking with two of his gang members. Candyman calls out to him. "I thought I told you to stay of out of my territory."

Trashman acting boldly. "And I told you I go where ever I please."

"Oh. You think you that bad?"

Bill and Buck place their hand on their pistol. Trashman takes notice. "You don't scare me." Buck fires a short into one of Trashman's member. Trashman and his other gang member raise their hands.

Candyman walks up to Trashman. "This is pay back for shooting my paper man." Tenants start moving away from the area.

Trashman is highly ticked off.

Candyman says, "You better pick up that piece of trash body you brought with you and leave before we shoot you and that other piece of trash."

"This is war you know."

"Call it what you want. The next any of you cross the line into our territory, you'll be getting a free ride out of here without your knowledge."

Trashman and his other member help the wounded member to leave the area. The other member says to Trashman. "Why you punken out?"

Trashman looks at him a little funny like. "You must be crazy. How you gonna deal with a pistol pointing into your face."

The next day Trashman and a half dozen members of his gang show up on the Miller Homes' ground. Candyman just happened to be sitting on the bench and see them coming. He gets up and starts running toward Tower One. Trashman and his gang open fire on Candyman. A hail of bullets fly all around him. He manage to reach the Tower, hits the ground, takes out his pistol and blindly starts firing back. Two of the stray bullets fired by Trashman gang hit an middle aged woman and a young girl trying to run away from the line of fire. The two are struck and drop to the ground. The woman moves slowly and stops. The young girl remains still. The firing stops. Trashman and his gang flee the area.

Moments later, the sound of a medic vehicle can be heard coming while tenants return to the court yard to investigate the shooting. Candyman comes to his feet and quickly goes into Tower One. The husband of the lady shot comes running from Tower Two. He sees the wife and child laying on the ground and rushes to them. The wife is not badly wounded, but the child has taken two hits and bleeding badly. Tenants start to gather around the fallen two. The medics arrive and rush to the victims. The police arrive and rope off the area while forcing the tenants to move back. The husband who is kneeing down beside his wife is removed by the police. The two victims are placed on a stretcher and taken away by the rushing medico vehicle.

Mark rolls a joint. He, Linda and Dee Dee are sitting on the couch, so call watching television. Linda is staring at Mark. He scene this and turns to look at her. "You know you're weird," he says. Dee Dee starts laughing.

"How so?" She asked Linda in a curious way.

"You lay with those guys on the street and come here wanting to lay with me."

Dee Dee looks at Linda. "Girl, I'm surprised at you. Ain't you got no respect?"

"There ain't no shame in my game. I like him more than you can imagine."

A news flash appeared across the television screen. Suddenly a news camera man appeared holding a microphone close to his face. "This just in from Miller Homes, the Center of Crime and Drugs in Trenton. The victims, a middle age women and a child has been shot here today. Their conditions are not known at this time." An elderly man approaches the camera man. The camera man hold the microphone down by his side and speaks low to the man. Suddenly the camera man pulls the microphone close to his face. "Sources are saying shootings have increased in and around this neighborhood since last year. This latest shooting may be tied to a shooting that took place around here last week. I have a tenant here who has seen a lot of shooting around here." He places the mic in front of the tenant's face. "Somebody from down town need to do something about these shooting before all of us are shot, beat up or killed. That little girl." He stops for a moment. "That little child didn't need that to happen to her nor did that lady."

Mark turns down the volume on the television. Casually, he smokes his joint. "I knew it. That's some of Trashman's doing. He would kill anybody just to be doing something. He is getting to be more and more dangerous."

Buck is sitting next to Candyman on Candyman's couch viewing the news report. Candyman turns off the television. "They keep saying the same thing. You see that? I don't know why they keep putting that mess on the screen."

Buck looked a little worried. "What we gonna do about Trashman, Candyman? We got caught up in this mess when Breeze got shot. You know the cops are out looking to get somebody."

Candyman is trying to play it off. "We do what we do best. Stay on the down low."

Buck feels good about Candyman's answer. "Yeah. That's the best way to deal with it for now. But Trashman got to be taken down."

The conversation goes cold. Suddenly Buck opened up. "We need to do this. Like break his back."

Bertha shows up for work at the beauty salon ready for work. She goes to her chair. A customer enters with no appointment. Bertha gladly invites the customer to sit in her chair. As soon as Bertha starts working on the lady's hair, Mark enters the salon and goes straight to Bertha's chair.

The co-worker sees Mark standing beside Bertha. "Ah, you're not welcome in here." Mark turns to her. "I didn't come to see you. Mind your own business."

Bertha steps into the conversation. "Please. Let me handle this. She takes money from her pocket and extends it to him. "Here Mark. Take this and leave." He starts walking toward the door.

The co-worker is furious. She calls out to him. "If I even see you walking pass this place again, I'm calling the police. And Bertha, if you still want to keep this job, you better choose better company."

Mark stops short of the door. "You think you bad. I'll deal with you later."

She shoots back. "Whatever you got, you better come correct because there will be something on this end waiting for you."

He gives her the finger and leaves by way of the front door.

Co-worker gets on the phone and starts dialing numbers. At the same time she is speaking to Bertha. "Keep him away from here or I'll have to fire you. You got that?"

Bertha just stares at her.

CHAPTER Six

Bertha goes to Sally's apartment after work. They sit in the front room. Bertha is upset about Mark coming to the salon and her cancer condition. Almost in tears, she feels the pain in her stomach. "I have been taking the medicines prescribed by my Doctor. It's not working that well."

"Maybe you should try seeing another Doctor as a second option."

"I thought about that. Monies' tight. They say marijuana helps both with the pain and healing."

"I wouldn't know. That's something maybe your doctor would know about."

"Yeah. guess you're right. And my other pain is my friend Mark. He almost caused me to lose my job today by coming in and causing trouble."

"How so?"

"By giving my co-worker a hard time."

"Maybe you should let him go."

"That would be hard to do. He's around when my son is not."

"Girl, you have to think what is best for you. Do you know which way is up?"

Trashman goes to Miller Homes looking for Mark to get the remaining money owed to him. He sees Breeze standing near a bench in the courtyard playing with a dog while his back is turned. Trashman walks up behind him and places his arm around Breeze's neck. "It's a dog-eat-dog world out here, dude. Just so happens you been in my territory a lot and that's a problem."

Breeze is barely able to breathe. He struggles to get loose. But Trashman keeps his hold in place.

Breeze is talking in a soft whisper. "You got this thing all wrong. I need to go to the drug store. That's my reason for being out there."

"Find another spot."

Breeze is twisting to free himself. "That's for my mom I'm talking about." Breeze starts to get mad. "You dissing my mom?"

Trashman sticks a gun into Breeze's ribs. "You ain't fooling no body carrying those papers. Let this be a warning to you. Stay out of my area. Next time might be your last trip there." He let Breeze loose.

Breeze goes straight to Candyman's apartment. Candyman is not happy with this news. "I got to get rid of him. Next time you go to the drug store, see me first. I got something for him."

Breeze shows a sign of relief.

Candyman gets serious. "We told you we got your back."

Bertha and Monique are sitting at the kitchen table. Monique leans over and says to Bertha, "Girl, what's happening to you? I thought when I helped you clean up that mess with Marcus years ago, you should have learned a lesson."

"Mark is really a nice person."

"Listen to me. Everybody knows he's no good. Just a pimp and hustler."

"I can't see it."

"You need to open your eyes. Even the people in the salon are talking bad about him and you. It's bad girl."

"Yeah. I know. He ain't going there no more."

"You don't get it." Monique starts to blow up. "You giving him money? Bertha I'm starting to feel sorry for you. You need to see a head shrink."

"I don't know. "I'm so all confused with this pain and all those other things going wrong all around me. Look at me. The Doctor got me taking treatments and pills. You got me smoking marijuana. One of my other friends want me to pray on it. Still the pain is here. Breeze fighting with Mark. Mark acting crazy half of the time. These things are beginning to make me half crazy as well."

"You got pains alright." Monique sees Bertha breaking down as she places her hand over her stomach and begins to frown. "What's wrong Bertha?" Now showing concern.

"It's my cancer. The doctor said I should be taking the prescribed medications and treatments to ease the pain." Bertha reaches out for the bottle and jar near the center of the table and shows them to Monique.

Monique takes them and quickly reads over both. "This is crap." She frowns. "I got something for that pain." She digs deep into her pocketbook and pulls out a healthy bag of marijuana. Places it on the table. "Here, take it. Don't worry about paying me for it. This place is loaded with it and I can get ALL I want."

Bertha looked at the bag. She twists her face up in pain. "I don't know. They say I should be taking what the Doctor ordered. They also say these pills will help my pain and act on the cancer."

"I ain't against Doctors, but you should still try this stuff in the bag. It's better than the other stuff I was giving you to smoke. Slightly stronger. It will make you feel good at the same time."

"Thanks. I'll try it later."

"And I'm telling you girl, you need to get yourself loose from that other mess. It's gonna get deeper if you don't bail yourself out now."

"I'll see what I can do."

"No. do it."

Trashman knocks on Mark's door. Linda opened it. He rushes in. Mark is watching television. He sees Trashman and jumps to his feet.

Trashman stops in front of Mark. He holds his hand out. "Where's my money?"

Mark is acting a little nervous. "I got it." He starts walking toward the bedroom.

Trashman calls out. "Make it quick. I ain't got all day and the money better be right."

Linda is sitting in a chair nearby winks at Trashman. "You wanna have some fun with me?"

Trashman gives her a dirty look. "I'm not your type."

"Oh yes you are. Big and strong. Nice looking, plenty of money."

"Knock it off. This is business."

Mark returns with a hand full of dollars. He hands them to Trashman. He does a quick count. Looks up at Mark. Not pleased. "This all you got?"

Mark starts to fear this man because he knows what this man is all about. "I can get more tomorrow."

Trashman pulls out his gun. "I'm tired of fooling around with you." He takes aim at Mark. Mark raises his hands and freezes. Trashman takes aim and fires a single shot into Mark's chest. Mark falls to the floor. Blood starts to appear on his shirt. Linda rushes to his body. Trashman looks down at him. "If you die. Debt paid. If you live, I'll be back and the next time will be your last day on earth if you don't have the rest of my money." He sticks his gun into his waist band, pulls his shirt over it and walks out the door, disappearing at the end of the hallway.

Mark is twisting his face in pain as he tries to speak to Linda in almost a low whisper. She draws her ear close to his face as tears drip onto him. "Call for help." In shock, she just stays near him crying. Mark passes out.

At the hospital, Mark is rushed into the operating room. Unconscious, slightly breathing. The bullet is removed and he is transported to a private room. Linda sits by his side as he slowly opens his eyes. She smiles. "I thought you was a goner."

"I didn't see it coming."

"And I didn't think he would do it. The shot scared me half to death."

Dee Dee enters the room. "Well, I see you been messing with the wrong person. Whoever it was, looks like they want die. My bad."

The Doctor enters the room. She looks at Mark. She goes to pull back a sheet covering his chest and touches parts of his body. Then plays with several feeders and writes something on a chart. She turns her attention to both ladies. "You got him here just in time. He lost a lot of blood. Now he needs rest. You should leave."

Dee Dee walks over to Mark. "These people out here don't play. When you get out of here, you better check yourself." Mark remains silent. She looks at the doctor. "Okay Doctor. I'm done." Both ladies leave the room. Mark closes his eyes.

The police are back at Miller Homes walking around trying to gather information about the latest shooting involving Mark from residents who may have heard or seen something.

Auntie is walking slowly towards her building when two police officers spot her. They walk swiftly to catch up with her. One cop walks beside her while the other lags slight behind. "Miss," he asked politely. "I see you around here a lot." They stop walking." "By any chance would you know anything about some of these shootings going on around here?"

"Sonny, I only come out here when I have too. I don't bother these peoples. What they do is their own business."

"Just thought you might have heard something."

She stares him straight in the face. "I ain't no stool pigeon. Don't be asking me anymore questions." She continued on her way.

The two cops see Bill sitting on a worn out bench while smoking a cigarette and looking down and toying with his cell phone. They walk up to him. He looks up when seeing a pairs of shoes in front of him.

"What's up?" Asked the light skin officer.

"Why you asking me?" Replied Bill. "You guys got all the answers."

"I wish we did. By the way. This guy that was shot the other day, was he from around here?"

"I don't know. I see him coming and coming from that building over there." He points to Tower One.

"Do you know who he hangs around with?"

"The only thing I know is that he sees some chick living there."

"What about you and your friends?"

"What about us?"

"Do you guys hang around with him sometimes?"

"Not really, I don't know the dude. Who shot him, I ain't got a clue."

"If you hear something, give me a call. The city is planning to offer a reward for information leading to his or her arrest." He takes out a card and hands it to Bill. The two police men walk away. Bill crushes up the card and placed it into his pocket.

Bill goes to Candyman's apartment. He tells Candyman what the cop said to him and shows him the card. Bill had an idea. "We could set Trashman up for the reward even if he didn't do it. This way we could get him out of our hair and make some extra doe."

Candyman is thinking. "No. I want that punk dead. I should have pulled the trigger when I had him down on the ground when he was in front of me. Besides, he and his boys tried to gun me down while I was out on the court yard. I ain't forgot about that. It's gonna be me or him."

Bertha heard about Mark through a news blast. She reported to work late. The ladies in the salon are giving her a funny look. Her co-worker stops working on a customer and looks in Bertha's direction. "Girl, I was wondering if you was coming back to work. Your customers are asking about you."

"Yeah, had to get some of my problems straightened out."

"I hope one of them was that 'what's-a-face' coming here to see you. I told my man friend about him. He got something for him the next time he sees him on the street."

"Oh. I guess you didn't hear. He was in a shooting and ended up in the hospital."

"No." Acting surprised. "I didn't hear about that. It's about time somebody put the hurt on him. He got me angary enough to want to hurt him myself."

Bertha was starting to get upset. "Well, he's in the hospital now doing well in recovering."

"With his attitude. What a shame. he should have died."

Bertha made no comment. She was starting to feel anger setting in. She started preparing her station for a scheduled customer. Just as she was finishing, her customer walks in. Bertha started working on her head. The customer is a resident of Miller Homes and had heard about the shooting. "That man who got shot over there at Miller Homes was a shame. I feel sorry for him. He has always been nice to me. That's a bad place to be."

Bertha was starting to feel a little better now that someone had something nice to say about Mark.

Weeks go by. Mark has mostly recovered from his near-death bout with Trashman. He was now back at his apartment almost able to function in a normal capacity. Linda and Dee Dee cleaned up the place and was now taking care of him. While he was away, both ladies had been working the streets and made enough money to pay off Trashman. Mark was glad. Now he could face Trashman debt free. But nothing came easy. He had to put up with Linda's nagging. She called herself getting even with him for the hard times he had been giving to her.

Several days after Mark's release, Bertha goes back to the hospital for another treatment. The Doctor tell Bertha, "It is too early to tell if the treatments are working. Are you taking the medicine that was prescribed?"

"Yes. But I'm not feeling any different when the pain comes back."

"I think I should prescribe a stronger dose for the one bottle. This should help with the pain."

"I hope so. This pain is wearing me down."

"Give it some time to work. Treating cancer is not an easy thing."

Trashman found out that Mark was out of the hospital. He went to see Mark to finish him off. To his surprise, Mark handed him all the cash owed and vowed not to deal with him again. However, in the back of him mind, he thought except for pay back in being shot.

Breeze had been by to see his mom several times during the weeks that passed. The paper route was paying off. He cleared his debt with Candyman and was getting her prescriptions filled while still living with Candyman.

Bertha went back to work only a couple days a week. Monique was dropping by to see if Bertha was using the marijuana she left with her. But in the past few weeks, Bertha's pain had gotten worse and she refused to let Monique enter her apartment.

On Monique's last trip to Bertha's, Monique refused to leave without see her. After Bertha could no longer take the pounding at her door, she let Monique enter.

"Why haven't you been letting me visit you?"

"I been spending most of my time in bed and I don't need company."

"Girl. You got to keep yourself active if you are to get over some of your problems."

"I know."

"I ain't going to stay. Just came to see if you was okay. I have to go now. But please open the door when I come. If you don't, I just might call 911."

"Okay. I still want us to be friends." She walked Monique to the door and they parted.

Because of her condition she was letting herself go down. With thin bags forming under her eyes, she looked at the ceiling with blood shot eyes. A police siren sound came through the light breeze window as the curtains swayed back and forth. Suddenly, there was a knock at the door. She went to answer it. Upon seeing Mark, she was not pleased. He stoles in with a black eye. She looks at him shocked. "What happened to you?"

"I ran into this dude who called himself a friend of the lady working at your salon shop. Me and him got into a beef and I put a hurting on him but I ended up with this black eye."

"You just don't know how to stay out of trouble."

"It seems to follow me everywhere I go."

"Speaking of problems. Everybody knows you're playing me. Even Breeze is thinking that."

"Baby, I ain't playing you."

"You coming around to see me and asking for money my son's given me to help get well."

"Baby, I need money too."

"I heard you got women out tricking and loading your pockets."

"It ain't like that. I had people on my back that I owed money too. Why do you think I got shot?"

"I don't know or care. You better hope my son don't find out you getting money from me. It's not gonna look good for me. And no telling what he might try to do to you."

"I ain't talking. Are you?"

"No, but the women at the salon are."

"I need to shut that big mouth lady up."

Bertha started showing a sign of anger. "Don't you be hurting them women!"

Mark starts feeling a little compassion. "I won't. I'm just talking."

"I'm gonna hold you to that."

Candyman increased Breeze's paper route to 50 customers. Breeze felt the increase was weighing him down with the extra load of papers. Instead of starting on the tenth floor as he would normally do, he started on the first floor and was working his way up. On the fourth floor, he knocks at a customer's door. The door opens and a young man greets him. "What's up dude," he asked.

"I'm the paper boy."

"Oh yeah. Well, I'll take one of them papers."

Breeze is not sure about this customer. "Um. These papers come with a price."

The young man looks around behind him and back to Breeze. "Okay. Come on in so you can get paid."

Breeze walks in. There're six guys sitting around the room. The door is closed behind him. Breeze starts to get nervous. The guy says to Breeze, "We know who you are and what you got. Give us those papers or we'll take them." Breeze starts heading for the door. Some of the group get up and rush to the door, blocking him from leaving. They grab one of his bags. He tries to hold onto it. One of the guys starts beating him in the face and chest. Breeze releases the bag in pain. More guys start beating on him while others tear open some of the papers. Finally, the guys get what they want. Breeze is taken to the door and thrown out into the hallway with only a few newspapers. Badly beaten, Breeze makes his way to Candyman's apartment. Candyman sees what has happened to him and flairs up. He tells the story to Candyman. Candyman becomes more outraged. He calls Bill and Buck to meet him in the courtyard with their gun.

Back at the apartment, the guys are sitting around joking, listening to music, and using the drugs. There's a knock at the door. At first the guys pay no attention to the knock. Then the knocks get louder. One of the young guys goes to open it. Candyman and his two boys rush in with guns in hand almost knocking down the door and guy to the floor. Candyman sees the newspapers in scraps around the floor.

"So, you dudes wanna have fun with MY paper boy." He, Bill and Buck point their pistols at the group. "Get up." Says Candyman. Those seated stand. "Get over to that wall." He points to the a wall he want them to stand next to with his gun. No one moved. One of them cry out. "I didn't do it." Candyman looks at him. "Shut up punk. Look at you. Power all around your nose. All of you in this together. You guys like beating up and robbing people. I got something for you. Empty you pockets on the table in front of you." Cash and other items come out. Bill and Buck pick through the pile and extract money and pocket it while Candyman keeps his gun trained on them. Candyman is not happy with the amount of money collected. For the last time he ordered them to go face the wall. "The first one to do something stupid, I ain't gonna think twice about shooting." They move to the wall. "Now face it." He nods to Bill and Buck to go beat on them. After the last two have been beaten and laying on the floor, Candyman walks over to them. "The next time my paper guy comes here, you better kiss his feet. Because if this happens again, you know the deal."

Trashman hears about Candyman ruffing up his guys. He and several gang members go to Miller Homes in search of Candyman. But he is nowhere to be seen.

Disappointed and angary, they robbed an elderly couple sitting on a bench. The couple try to fight back in protest but Trashman and his guys produce guns that made the couple give in. Trashman made them a promise that he and his guys will return if they cause any trouble. Not caring about their feeling, he and his guys walk away from the area. The couple walk away as if nothing had happened. This was not their first encounter with Trashman and his gang.

Breeze returned to Bertha's apartment. Bertha is not pleased after seeing Breeze's bruises. However, she does not question him and he makes no comment.

Several weeks later, another meeting was being held with the mayor. This time he presented a plan to help reduce crime around Miller Homes. "I have talked with the police chief and he is sending two shifts of police officers to patrol that area. They will be working during the evenings and nights."

Bertha, who has been standing in the rear of the room steps into the center isle. The mayor sees her and stops talking.

Bertha raises her hand to speak. He points to her. "Mr. Mayor. Are these officers going to enforce the law? Or are they just there for show?"

"We never put officers on show. They will strictly enforce the law."

"That's what the mayor before you said."

An elderly couple stood. The man raised his hand. The mayor pointed to him. "We just want to see justice. We tired of being robbed while out in that courtyard. And those little kids need a place to play. When you gonna fix up that play ground."

"As your mayor, I'm gonna be working to make Miller Homes a better place."

Bertha pointed toward the mayor. "Prove it to us by starting your plan tomorrow."

The crowd agreed. Someone in the back yelled out. "YEAH. DO IT."

The mayor walked off the platform and left the meeting.

Weeks go by. Monique makes another trip to check on Bertha. Bertha has been holding out on being seen around the grounds. Monique parks herself on the couch where she usually sits. Bertha is coming out of the kitchen where she picked up the bag of marijuana Monique left for her. She placed the bag on the coffee table. Monique looks at it. "Bertha. You haven't touch it. Why?"

"I'm not sure this is going to help my condition."

"Well, how did you feel when we were smoking it together when I was here before?"

"Oh. I felt good. But shortly after you left. It wore off and the pain returned. I can't smoke this every time I feel pain. I just can't function like that. What is my son going to say when he sees me lighting up and getting high all the time?"

"Girl I was only trying to give you advice and help you with your pain."

Monique buried the bag in her pocket book. "You know they missing you at the salon. You plan on going back?"

"Yeah. Breeze can't handle all my bills by himself. Plus him working them two jobs, I know it's got to be hard on him."

Monique perks up and looks Bertha straight into her eyes. "Breeze ain't working two jobs?"

Bertha becomes shocked into Surprise. "What are you talking about?"

"You don't know? Mark introduced him to Candyman the drug king who operate the drug business around here. He quit his job to make more money by working for him so he could be better help to you."

Bertha places her hand over her breast. "No. Not my Breeze. Selling drugs?"

"You could say that. He's doing the newspaper route."

"Mark said something about Breeze having a paper route, but he made it sound like it was a honest paying job."

"You have to be careful about hearing what he's tell you. You can't trust Mark in telling you all the right stuff. Girl. We living in a different world now. You need to wake up and smell the roses. You mean to tell me with all the money Breeze is bring home, you don't know what he's doing?"

"Monique. What should I do? He's helping me with my bills. If I get on him and make him stop. What do I do next?"

"For the time being, I wouldn't say anything until you can work out another plan."

"Maybe you're right. I can't take any more bad news. I just can't." She starts to cry. Monique places her hand on Bertha's arm.

"Get Mark alone and ball him out."

"Yeah. That I can do. I don't want Breeze to destroy his future."

Bertha has been holding up in her apartment for over two weeks. Today she is going out onto the courtyard just to get some fresh air. Upon entering the area, she sees Sally sitting on an old park bench. Their eyes meet and bertha walks over and sits beside her.

"My goodness," says Sally. "Where have you been? It has been awhile since we was last together."

"Oh. I have been taking care of my personal problem. Like getting my treatments and trying to work when my condition permits."

"How are the treatments coming along?"

"To be truthful, they are not working too well. And the pills, they do help a little."

"Have you tried seeing another doctor?"

"No. My son is working and with me working part time, we just don't have the funds to reach out like that. I have been smoking a little marijuana every now and then. It does help with the pain and it takes my mind off of my condition."

"Well, all I can do for you is pray that things get better before they get worse."

"Thanks. And speaking of worse. You know I have a lot of old memories in my head that won't seem to go away."

"Tell me about it. I like hearing old stories."

"It was this teenager who lived next door to me when I was about six years old that I called him by his street name which I can't remember to this day. Anyway one day the sky turned dark during the day light hours. I mean it had gotten so dark that it seemed black. It had gotten so dark that the street lights came on. People thought the world was coming to an end. The next door guy was always down on the avenue hanging around on the corner. I heard a loud bang while I was sitting on my porch coming from down on the avenue. Someone came up the street yelling somebody had gotten shot. Later, it just so happened that the guy next door was the one who was shot dead in a drive-by shooting."

"That's awful," said Sally with a sad looking face.

"As I was about to say, back in those days, not many people had locks on their doors. I would go in and out of his house often. Well, I remember seeing some men dressed in black carrying this long fancy box into his house and a lot of people dressed up in the same color clothing going in to visit. So, the next morning when nobody was around, I went into the house to see what everybody was coming to see in the box. I saw him lying in the box in front of the front room window all dressed up. I went back home quickly. Being a little kid at the time, I didn't give it a thought. It may have been two or three days later, some of those same people came back and took the box away in this long black car. I saw several cars loaded with people following this long black car until it got out of sight. No one ever said a word to me about him."

"That must have been weird to see coming from a child's eye sight."

"Now it seems funny that back in those days, viewing were held in people's homes. And it must have been an ordeal getting that box into the house and setting it up by the front room window."

"That would make me wonder also."

"My friend Mark got shot and that's what brought back that memory."

"Guess you know we can't stay out here too long. Them gangs are always coming through here. I heard about that couple who was out here just catching some fresh air and was robbed by a gang. I think that's awful when you have to be afraid to leave your apartment. The mayor keeps telling us he's going to provide security for us, but when. I haven't seen any real security since living here."

"You saw how he walked away from the meet. And before telling us the police force doesn't have the man power to send officers to Miller Homes. Why because they are all up in the high class people's area. Don't look for any real change. It just ain't gon'na happen."

The mayor is sitting behind his desk talking on the phone with the police chief. "I think this thing about the Miller Homes has gotten too far out of hand and we need to do something, quick."

The chief on the other end is not agreeing with the mayor. "We have been trying for year to rid that place of crime. The people are complaining but they won't point to who the bad persons are. I have been sending officers over there and the people just seem like the officers are bothering them. I haven't had one tenant to give us any information or point out who is troubling them. I'm not sure if I send the two shifts of officers over there, things are going to get any better. I think we should just tear the place down to end the problems. The news media has already given Miller Homes a bad wrap by calling it "Killer Homes."

The voices on the phone went silent for a few seconds. The mayor was given thought to what the chief had said. "Maybe you have a point there. If I can got the city council to tear the buildings down, we would be breaking up that crowd by displacing all those tenants back into the city and else where. I think that would make it harder for the gangs and drug dealers to operate."

"You're the mayor. Speak to the council and try to get them to agree with you."

Bertha is in Sally's apartment. "Yeah. I would like to talk longer, but I need to go and get ready for work. You know how the customers get fidgety when you don't show up to work on time."

"Know what you mean. I won't hold you. And try to take better care of yourself."

"I will."

The next morning Breeze goes out on his route. He knocks on the door of one of Tower Two's apartment. A lady answers the door. She looks as if she is high on something. Her words come out in a slur. "What can I do for you Sonny?"

"I'm the paper boy."

She staggers as she pulls the door wide open and waves for Breeze to enter. The place is messy with thing laying everywhere. He steps over a few items as he enters the apartment.

"You got a paper for me?"

He double checks the list. "Yeah. Here's your paper."

She takes it. Takes the drugs out and hands the paper back to him. He's puzzled. He looks at her. "Where's the money?"

"Oh. I don't have any. You want to have fun with me?"

"Lady. This is business. If you can't pay, I need the drugs back."

"You gave me the paper. So everything in it is mind."

He reaches for the drugs. She pulls back. He grabs her arm. She tries to shake loose. "I'll call the cops if you don't let me go."

"Wait till Candymen hears about this."

"I like that sound. C a n d y m a n. He must be someone sweet."

Breeze leaves. He finishes the route and reports to Candyman. Candyman thinks for a moment. "Okay. Forget about her. Just take her off the list. When I put her on, I thought she was gonna be trouble. If it would have been any body other than her, I would go over there and bust them up."

"Sorry I gave her the paper before she gave me the money."

"Don't worry. Things happen. This ain't the first time I had this problem with her."

Breeze gives Candyman the money he collected and receives his cut.

A few days later, Breeze moves back to Bertha's apartment still showing light battle scares around his face. Bertha takes notice but is afraid to ask about how they came to be.

The next morning Breeze goes out on his route delivery and comes back to do his favorite thing, watch cartoons.

Bertha could no longer hold it in. Something was eating at her and she had to confront him. "Son, I see you haven't been going to you job lately."

"Yeah, mom. Me and the boss couldn't make it together. I thought it was best I quit before I got mad enough to break his face."

"That's not good. I notices some light scares on your face that wasn't there weeks ago."

Breeze starts to feel a little uneasy. "Mom, what's this, 20 questions?"

"No, just a little concerned about you."

"I'll be okay."

Bertha returned to work. Her co-worked watches as she sets up her area in preparation to work on customers.

"I see you decided to come back to work."

"Girl, you don't know the problems I have been dealing with. But things are starting to get a little better."

"Hope you got rid of the crazy guy who was coming around here looking for money and causing trouble?"

"Sore of. I stopped giving handouts."

Auntie comes in the salon. She sees Bertha and goes to her chair. "Girl, I had a long day and I need something done with this mop of mind." She starts running her fingers threw her hair. The ladies in the salon laugh. Bertha smiles. "Auntie, you come to the right place. I can make you look like a princess."

Auntie smiles. "Oh no. I don't want to look that good. I don't want them young fellows chasing after me." The ladies continue to laugh. Bertha starts working on her hair.

"You know this young kid name Candyman?"

Bertha pauses. "Sort of. What's so special about him."

"He was my nephew's best friend. After my nephew left town, he started coming to see me and has been helping me with things every since. He's such a nice kid."

Bertha had other thoughts. In her mind she was thinking, *'He's a drug dealer and thug. I don't know why she can't see it.'* "As long as he is helping, that's really great."

Auntie does a slight twist around in the chair. "Why don't you and your boy come for dinner and meet him. I'm sure you'll like him."

"Auntie. I have a very busy schedule. I would like that but I'm too busy at this time. Maybe some other day would be good."

"I hope so."

CHAPTER Seven

Bill and Buck had papers left over from their paper route. Instead of returning them to Candyman, they decided to sell them on the street to people they thought they could trust. While walking the streets in Trashman's territory, they was spotted by some of Trashman's gang. Out numbering Candyman's guys by their gang size, the gang decided to rob them of their papers. The two under attack became defenseless. They run off after losing the papers. Trashman's gang decide to sell the papers to people they knew from being around them not sure of their trust. As they started selling the papers, people who knew what the paper business was about all about gladly purchase them as the gang continue selling them until all were sold out.

Candymen was later told about what Trashman's gang had done. As for punishment for working out of territory and not returning the extra papers, he cut them off from delivering to their route and would go after Trashman to settle the score.

One of the purchasers who was a longtime friend of one of Trashman's gang members wanted to purchase a dozen papers in a package deal under a bridge next to a canal that next evening. An agreement was made and the person left satisfied. They would give this news to Trashman.

The gang immediately went to see Trashman with this good news. Trashman thought it was a great idea. But there was one problem. Where to get the papers from. Candyman was not willing to give up the papers to a bunch that was making life difficult for him and his gang. One member came up with a bright idea. Several of them would go up to the fourth floor of Tower One. Wait for the paper boy and rob him. "Great idea," said Trashman.

The next morning the gang went to Tower One. They waited in the hallway on both sides of the fourth floor door way leading into the hallway. As Breeze entered the hallway, the gang immediately grabbed him, taking all his papers. Being out numbers, Breeze ran down the stairs and out of the building.

That evening, the plan was to go off as scheduled. Trashman told two of his gang members to hang back and watch for anybody that might want to start some action. He also, had another member to stay back with the papers in case the deal went bad. He and the remaining gang started walking until reaching the directed place. It was nearing dark by now. Street lights flicker over their heads. As he and his guy head towards the bridge, Trashman received a cell phone call from their connections telling them the bridge was up a head if Trashman was not sure if this was the right bridge. The voice on the other end told him he was heading toward the right place. A gray pickup truck sat under the bridge. A lone undercover cop was sitting on the passenger seat with the door opened and his legs hanging down. Trashman and gang members went up to the pick-up truck. There was a short discussion between Trashman and the man. The deal was not going according to Trashman's liking. The man was acting funny by asking a lot of questions. The man would not part from the truck. Trashman told his guys to surround the truck and for the man to move over. He climbs in next to the driver. As the undercover cop did so, Trashman asked to see the cash. He pulled a bag out from under the seat. Then the man asked to see the papers. Trashman gave him a dance and song story. The man continued to hold the bag. Suddenly there was a shot fired in the truck. Trashman climbed down from the truck. Three undercover cops appeared from hidden places and start firing at the group. One gang member dropped dead while Trashman and the others dropped to the ground firing back. All three cops were shot dead after being caught in a cross fire from the three guys who were holding back. Trashman walked up to one of the dead bodies. He started checking his pockets. He found a badge and wallet in one pocket. He opened the wallet and looks through it while his gang watched on. It was empty except for a police badge and two twenty dollar bills. Trashman started scoffing. "Should've known he was a cheap scape. Forty bucks." He picked up the bag the man was still holding. It was full of paper. Trashman became very angary at this point. "He didn't plan on buying the papers. It was a setup."

One of the gang member held out his hand. "I'll take the twenties if you don't want them."

Trashman looked at him as if he was crazy. He placed the badge and money into his own pocket and turned a couple of the bodies over. "Look at these ugly piece of good for nothing. They didn't know this was gonna be their last day." Trashman looked at gang. "I thought these narcs would be targeting Miller Homes. How'd they catch a scent of us?"

One of the members shrugged his shoulders. "No clue. Probably one of the gang members was trying to set up a deal, so he called you in."

Trashman turned to the group. "This is messed up. Don't be making deals unless you know the dude. Got that?"

The group had nothing to say.

Cangyman changed his mind about taking Bill and Buck off the job. He gave them Breeze's routes and told them to be armed at all times because Trashman was out of his mine and dangerous. Bill and Buck was making the rounds during the evening because they liked sleeping late in the morning.

The mayor could no longer take the pressure of Miller Homes tenants giving him a hard time about their safety with the rising crime building up in the area. He made a deal with the police chief to add additional funding to the police force in order to add security for Miller Homes. And so it happened.

The two evening undercover police officers tried to be less conspicuous as possible by pretending to be visiting friends living in the Miller Homes area. At the same time they were on the lookout for the gang and drug dealers. They spotted Bill and Buck standing next to Tower Two smoking marijuana. They approached Bill and Buck. The officers grab Bill and Buck by their arm. Bill and Buck look confused. A police car rolls up on the lot. The brown skin officer points his gun at Bill and Buck. "Drop down on your knees and place your hands on the back of your head." There was a look of defeat on their face. Bill looked at Buck as he tries to break free from the officer's grip. The other officers held him tight and threw him flat to the ground. The brown skin officer kicks Bill a few times. Bill squirms in pain. Buck looked at the other officer in fear. He begs. "Why you picking on us?" The other officer points a gun at him without saying a word. Buck put his hands in the air. The brown skin officer made Bill stand. Both Bill and Buck follow the command. The officers made them knee long enough to place them in hands cuffs behind their backs. Shortly after, they were placed into a car and taken way.

Bertha was in her apartment with thin bags under her eyes wide awake looking toward the ceiling through blood shot eyes. Mark was sitting beside her on the couch. Police sirens was sending out ragging sounds in the back ground.

KNOCK. KNOCK. KNOCK. Could be heard coming through the siren ragging pass the kitchen window. Bertha knows it is not Breeze because he has a key. Bertha hears the door shaking as Monique twist and turn the outside handle. The door doesn't open.

Monique is calling from the hallway outside Bertha's door. "Bertha. We need to talk."

Mark leaves the front room and goes into the bedroom.

Bertha exhales in relief. She walks to the door and opens it. Monique wears a warried look in her face. "I haven't seen you since the last time we talked. Why haven't you answered my calls? And what for God sake is that smell?" The apartment has not been kept up.

Monique looks around and sees unwashed dishes in the sink. Trash scattered over the floor. And roaches feasting on left overs. Bertha picks up a garbage bag and places some trash on the floor into the bag. "Sorry 'bout the mess. I've been uh, busy."

Monique shows concern. "Busy doing what? Have you been here all day? Don't you have to go to work?"

Bertha goes and shove clothes off the couch. "Why don't you-ah-have a seat?"

Monique looks at her even more worried and confused. "What have you been on. You look terrible."

Mark, shirtless, comes out of the bedroom. Monique's jaws drop. "Who is this?"

"This is Mark. He's a friend."

Monique stares at Mark. "I heard about you, but this is my first time actually seeing you." She turns to Bertha. "Can I talk to you in private?"

Mark just looks at her, doesn't say a word and walks off into the bathroom closing the door behind him.

The two walk into the bedroom. Remnants of drugs are on her bed. Monique picks them up. She shakes her head while holding them up to Bertha's face. "Have you been doing drugs?"

Bertha looking all wide eyes. She hesitates to speak. "No."

"What's this I see in front of me? You said you wasn't into this stuff. I gave you marijuana which is better for you. Girl this is all wrong from what I see."

Bertha shakes her head. "No. They're not mine. They're his." She scratches herself in an anxious manner.

Monique whispering. "Lord Jesus, Bertha you need help. That man outside is bad news. You of all people should know better than that. When it comes to picking male friends, you seem to fall over board and lose your sense of what's right. "

"He's been helping me. I can see the good in him."

Furious Monique tries to compose herself. "Are you serious? Helping you with what? This?" She holds the drug parts up closer to bertha's face. "Where is Breeze? Do he know you and your so call friend fooling around with this stuff?"

"He just returned home a couple of day ago. He's out right now. He don't come into this bedroom."

"I can't believe this. You was the one who said this place wasn't safe for any child. Bertha, girl, I'm so mad that you ain't learning nothing. Nothing. Nothing." She stomps her feet. "I'm sorry but you need real help."

Bertha holds up her hands. "Let me explain."

Monique takes out her phone and starts dialing a number. Bertha swipes at the phone in her hand.

Monique is holding tight to it. "What on earth are you doing?"

Bertha is hand wrestling with Monique and is able to take the phone way. "Monique. This cancer seems to be getting worse."

Monique had forgotten about Bertha's cancer. She drew back some of her anger. "And I suppose you think this guy is good for you?"

"You can't tell anybody able this. Okay?"

"On what place of God's green earth did you think it was okay to bring an addict into your life?"

Water starts running from Bertha's eyes. "I can't work. I'm in constant pain. Breeze does what he can with the paper route. And he's here to help pay for the medicine and…"

Monique is disappointed. "I'm sorry. Cancer or not. This is no way to live."

"I'm sorry. I have trouble helping myself."

Monique walked into the kitchen. Bertha follows. Monique goes to the refrigerator to get herself something to drink. Upon opening it, a sour smell fills the air. Items that have been sitting there for weeks had lost their original color. Monique immediately closes the refrigerator door and retreats to the kitchen table. She is infuriated but does not try to let it show. "You don't know that world your child is living in. Being the newspaper boy with that type of route, he's taking a chance every time he delivers those papers. Everybody knows he's been shot at least once and problem threatened or beat up once if not more times. It's a tuff job. I hope for your sake that he can stay safe on that job until your sickness clears up."

Bertha, who had been looking out the kitchen window sees two guys (whom she knows) Bill, Buck getting into a parked police car's back seat with another young man.

Mark comes out of the bathroom. "Looking for your kid? I saw him walking around here carrying papers. The cops were following him. I think they might be on to him."

Bertha grabs both sides of her face and runs out the door and down the stair case with the sound of her heart beating in her ears.

Monique rushes out of the apartment yelling from above the stairs.

"Bertha! Bertha, wait."

The sound of Bertha's 'THUMP. THUMP. THUMP can be heard running down the three flights of stairs. This was causing her to pant heavily. She ran out of the building, sweat dripping from her hair. She looked around in panic looking at every face getting into police cars. The brown skin police officer walked up to her. Monique trailing behind the both of them. Bertha felt his presents and turned to face him.

"Is there a problem ma'am?"

Bertha was deep in thought and doesn't quite hear him. "Huh? What?" Her eyes meets his gaze.

The officer looks at her suspiciously.

She is stunned by his speech. "No. No. I was just looking for my son."

"Is he anyone of these boys?"

Bertha looks into the vehicle at Bill and Buck and the others. No, I don't see him."

"Good." The officer turns his back on her and walks to another police car. He enters the car and it drives away.

Breeze walks up behind her and taps her on the shoulder. She jolts from the touch and the sound of his voice. "Mom."

Bertha turns around and hugs Breeze tightly. Tears flow from her eyes. "I thought you was going to jail." She starts pleading with him. "Please stay with me. Don't leave like you did before."

He looks into his mother's eyes. "I won't go if you make Mark leave." He sort of pulled himself away from her. "Why did you think I was going to jail?"

"I know you quit your office job and I know all about you working for Candyman. But its alright."

He became surprised. "Who told you about Candyman and what I am actually doing?"

"Son I know everything."

Breeze started showing signs of anger. "No. Tell me who told you. Tell me?"

"Son. It wouldn't make any difference."

"It was Mark wasn't it. It had to be him. He got a big mouth. Wait till I see him." He raised his fist. "I got something for him."

Bertha didn't want to see them get into a fight. "It wasn't him. It was one of my girlfriends."

With the help of some of their friends, Bill and Buck were able to be released from jail on bail. They returned to Miller Homes just in time to find Trashman and a few of his gang members showing up at the same time. Tenants out in the courtyard saw this as being a sign of trouble. They quickly gathered up their kids and retreated inside their building. Bill and Buck walked out to meet Trashman and his gang. Bill stepped up to Trashman. "You know you out of place coming around here." Buck punched one hand into the other. Meaning he was ready to start something. One of Trashman's boys saw this and threw a punch at Bill and a fight was on. Trashman backed away to let them get it on. Bill and Buck were out-numbered and was quickly beaten to the ground.

Trashman called out to Bill and Buck who were laying on the ground. "Tell that punk Candyman, he's next." He and his gang went into Tower One and disappeared. Suddenly, several police cars arrive while the two are picking themselves up from the concrete. A couple came out of Tower Two pointing the police in the direction of the two while telling them about the fight.

The police pack them into a car and drive away.

The rest of the day was still. No outsiders on foot came to buy drugs. Very few cars came and left the parking lot. Just the faint sound of glass shattering and people yelling from their apartment.

Night fell and Mark returned to Bertha's apartment. Silhouettes of Bertha and Mark fighting shown through the apartment window. Mark starts throwing dishes and furniture all over the place in a rage. Bertha, exasperated and crying pleas with him. "Please, Mark, just leave." He pays no attention to her. She runs to her phone and instantly picks it up. "Leave or I'll call the cops!"

Mark looks really furious. "They don't scare me. Fine. If you want it that way. Don't expect any more money from me when Breeze can't help you. You'll be dead soon. I can see none of that crap you taking is helping." He walked out of the apartment.

Breeze knocks on Candyman's door. Candyman opens it looking tired. "Oh, it's you. Come on in."

Breeze walked in just far enough for Candyman to close the door. "I won't be long," he says.

"I'm tired and need to get some shut eye. What's on your mind."

"I can't be delivering anymore."

"Okay. I can see it."

"Yeah. I've been shot, beat down and giving a hard time by people who don't even like me. I can't see dying while trying to make good money. It just ain't worth it."

"Okay."

"I need to take care of my mom."

"Okay."

"You're not mad?"

"Half my crew are in jail. What am I going to do?"

"I'm sorry, Candyman."

Candyman looks down hearted. "Just look out for yourself, kid. Don't get into any trouble."

At home. The television is on. Breeze is sitting and watching while leaning forward on the couch. Bertha is in the kitchen frying four eggs, potatoes and placing toast in the toaster. Breeze's program is interrupted by a brief news report. A reporter appears on the screen holding a microphone to his face. "Miller Homes continues to be on tight watch. A total of five drug dealers were put under arrest yesterday after tenants complained about gang violence and selling drugs to kids. Two arrested during the day and three arrested later in the evening." A camera transfer to a showing of Bill and Buck being placed into a police car and a later view of three others being handcuffed and placed into a wagon. The camera man returns. "Suspects are being held in the downtown police station. Without proper evidence, suspects may be released within 24 hours."

Bertha is watching from the kitchen. "It's the same old thing. Police ain't properly doing their job when you need them to do it. Always arresting the wrong people and letting the real criminals and drug lords roam free. Just for once I'd like to see them arrest a white person. No, it's always somebody black."

Breeze was just mumbling loud enough so his mom could hear him. "They ain't got nothing on Bill and Buck. They were carrying weed and in several fights."

Bertha places the food on the table. She didn't catch all of what he was saying.

"What was that baby? Come to the table."

"Nothing much. Just calling it as I see it."

Breeze sits down at the table across from him. "You know what?" She stops and is thinking.

Breeze wants to know what's on her mind. "What?" He takes two of the eggs, a piece of toast and a few potatoes and starts eating.

After a short pause she brightens up. "We should get out of here."

Breeze stops eating and looks up to her. "What do you mean?"

"I mean this time move to your gran mama's place." Breeze smiles. A moment of silence is present while they eat. "You'll love it at mama's. Fresh air every day. And none of this mess that's going on around here."

Breeze is surprised. "Really. We can go?" Acting boyish.

"Yeah. And you could probably go to college."

He starts beaming at her. "And we'd find a way to get you better."

Bertha starts to put on a smile. "Yeah."

Bertha walked into the salon. She begged her boss for her job back.

Her boss is not happy with her. "Bertha, since you been here, we been having more trouble than we need around here."

Bertha has that sad look about her. "It really ain't my fault. Those people seem to pick me out of thin air. You see I do good work and my customers like me."

"What about your health? Can I depend on you to work without falling down on the job or running out every time something happens?"

"Yeah. I need this job to pay for my medicine."

"Okay. I'm going to let you stay. Just remember what I just said." She placed a finger up close to Bertha's face. "Just keep those no good boy friends of your out of here."

"No problem. I'm through with that mess."

One of Bertha's customers come in. "Girl, I thought we lost you. Can you do my hair?"

"Sure. The chair is all yours." The lady picks a magazine from a rack and parks her body onto Bertha's chair. Bertha starts working on her hair, and continues doing manicure and pedicure. The work is finally completed. The lady take a long look in the mirror and smiles. "Fine job." She gives Bertha the payment and a tip and heads for the salon exit. "See you in a couple of weeks," she says as she exit without looking back. Bertha is pleased. She smiles to her boss. Boss looks up from doing another customer's hair. No words to be said, just a smile in return.

Bertha goes to the drug store and buys her own medicine. She feels good about being able to help herself. As she walks along the street, a car pulls up close to the curb and moves at her walking pace. A guy sitting next to the window rolls it down. She looks to see its Mark. She starts walking a little faster. The car speeds up to keep up with her. "Bertha," he says in a soft voice. She doesn't look in his direction. He hangs both arms over the open window. He tries again. "Hey baby. I miss you."

She looks at him. "You miss the money I was giving you."

"Don't talk like that. We had a good thing. Why you want to end it like this?"

"Leave me alone. Go talk that mess to your other lady friends."

"They just business partners." The car comes to an intersection and stops with two cars a head of his. Bertha steps up a little faster and walks around the corner before the light changes and ducks into a store. The light changes and the car rolls around the same corner. Mark has lost Bertha from view. The car stops. Mark gets out and starts walking, looking for her. She sees him passing the store while standing behind a clothing rack moving clothes from one side to the other. She wait for a moment, then exits the store and walks back around the corner heading toward the salon. Once inside the salon, she makes a phone call. Her co-worker is cleaning up. Bertha helps while waiting for Breeze to come. Bertha says to her co-worker. "You can't even walk the streets without these crazy guys wanting to talk to you."

"Know just what you mean. I had to bust one of them in the head for putting his hand on me. They getting outrageous. They think they own us."

"I read in the newspaper a few weeks back that some lady shot one of them for acting crazy. If it gets any worse, us women might have to go into hiding."

Her co-work looked at her. "I'd leave this town first." That was Bertha's plan but she didn't want to tell her just yet.

Breeze comes into the salon. She stops working and together they walk to the apartment.

After entering the apartment, Breeze turns on the television. The news channel is tuned in. A board caster is giving an up data on Miller Homes. Breeze calls out to his mom who is in the kitchen washing dishes. "Mom come here. They're talking about the Miller Homes." She comes to hear what is being reported. She takes a seat on the couch.

"Miller Homes is now under police watch stemming from a gang war where a lady and little girl have been shot. The two victims have been taken to a Trenton Hospital where they are in stable condition and are expected to recover." Breeze changes the channel. Bertha says to Breeze. "This is why we need to move away from here. Things are getting worse and who knows, we might be next."

"How we gonna make it without either of us working and that small check you getting from the government?

The phone rings. She goes to look at the caller ID. It's the hospital. She answers it. On the other end is her doctor. "Bertha?" she ask.

"Yes. This is she."

"I have some good news for you. After looking at your negatives, we believe we can remove the cancer tissues causing you pain. Would you be willing to come in so we can take another look?"

Berthe is excited. "Sure. When?"

"Next Tuesday at 9 a.m."

"Sure. I'll be there." She hangs up the phone. She gives Breeze the good news. He is all excited as well.

The following week Bertha reports to the hospital. She goes through a series of test and is released. The following week she is called in for an operation. Breeze goes with her and waits in the waiting room for the results. Hours later, the Doctor come to Breeze and tells him the operation went well and they should know if they removed everything when they do their next test. Breeze leave with a good feeling.

Bertha remained in the hospital for two weeks. After that time, she becomes well enough to go home. Breeze thought it best that he go back to doing the paper route because there was very little money coming in through Bertha's government assistance check. So now, he is doing the paper route and the remaining time caring for his mom.

A week later, the phone rings. Bertha looks at the caller ID. It's the hospital. She answers. The voice on the other end ask? "Bertha?"

"This is she."

"This is your doctor. I have good news and some not so good news. The good news is that we were able to remove most of the cancer causing problem. However, we was not able to remove all of it. However, you should not be having any serious pain. That's a good thing. However, you will have to continue treatments.

Hopefully, the small remaining area will go away with the treatments and medications."

Bertha felt the news really wasn't all that good, but for the time being she felt better as long as the pain was gone. When Breeze arrived at home, she told him what the doctor had said. He felt good that something had been done and he could now sleep at night.

Mark's Cousin with the same tattoo and Candyman's cousin around Breeze's age sat smoking meth in Mark's apartment. Mark's Cousin placed his pipe over an ash tray. His face turned sour. His thoughts went back to his cousin. He visualized what happened to him. "Trashman killed my cousin a few years back. I was there to see him overdose on meth. His eyes were glassy looking at the ceiling and suddenly he passed out. He was just a kid dealing for Trashman. Then Trashman got nervous and tried to wake him, but he was gone. Trashman started sweating profusely. So, we put my Cousin's body in a black garbage bag and took it down to the river and pushed it off the bridge into the river."

Mark shook him to bring him back to the present. But he was on a roll and had to get it out. "Yeah. He threw my cousin down the river. Trashman started smoking a cigarette as we looked at the body as it started riding the current and sank. Next few days my aunt called me to tell me the authorities found his body tangled in some trash on the edge of the river."

Mark put a solemn look on his face. His cousin looked at him with a hint of remorse. "That hurt me to my heart." Liquid started forming under his eyes.

Bill held his head down low.

Cousin wiped the tears away. "That's why he doesn't do drugs. After that, he just started hurting and harassing people like taking their money and beating up on them."

Mark banged his fist on the coffee table. "It doesn't matter. He thinks he can get away with everything. The people around here fear him. On the other hand, Linda and Dee Dee ain't bringing in enough money. I don't know why I'm telling you this. He almost took me out over a debt. We need to stop him. He's getting more and more crazier. If you wanna work for me you have to earn my trust."

"What kind of work are you talking about?"

"I need people to watch out for my two girls so Trashman don't be trying to hustle them. I'd love to see him either in prison or dead."

Cousin was quick to respond. "I got you boss. Anything to get that crook out of the way. If I see him around them ladies, I might just take him out myself."

Mark started walking away mumbling. "Prove it by help doing it." He walked out of the apartment, out of Tower One, around the edge of the Tower and disappeared still mumbling to himself.

While he was out walking, he starts thinking about the problems he has been having with the lady in the salon. He makes his way to the salon. The salon was packed with ladies. He goes inside. The co-worker immediately spots him. He goes straight up to her. "I hear you been bad mouthing me. And that man friend of your called himself stepping to me. I had to put him in his place."

"Yeah. You're nothing but a piece of trash."

He punches her in the face. She fall back against the item shelf and grab a curling iron only to come back at him with a mighty force. He blocks it and delivers another blow to the upper area of her chest. She drops the curling iron and begins to start coughing as she falls to the floor. One of the other workers runs up behind him with a small metal trash can and whacks him across the back of his head. He falls and two of the ladies start kicking him. The co-worker is able reach into apron and dial 911.

A police car patrolling the area not far away rushes to the salon and arrest Mark. Two days later, Linda and Dee Dee bail him out of jail. The three of them are sitting on the couch. Dee Dee says to Mark. "You like starting trouble I see." Mark is laying back on the couch. "She had it coming. If all those ladies was not there, I would have finished her off."

"Well, looks like you got the raw end of the deal."

"Yeah. But she knew I meant business."

"And she probable meant to hurt you as well."

The next day Bertha goes to the salon. Her co-worker is working on customer with a bruise on her face. She sees Bertha coming in. She stops working on the customer and excuses herself. She meets Bertha half way into the salon. "Girl. Your man friend or that piece of trash came in here and started beating on me. Like I said before. We don't need that kind of trouble around here. As of right now, you don't work here anymore."

"I'm sorry all this happened. I just came in to say I quit and wanted to pick up all my stuff."

"You're welcome to it. I was really starting to like you and so was the ladies here. I wish things didn't have to end this way, but I have a business here and I want to keep it that way."

"I understand," She collected her items and the other girls waved as she was leaving.

Candyman goes into Trashman's area looking for him. As he drives up close to where Trashman is standing, Trashman recognizes the BMW and opens fire on him. Bullets rip through the vehicle without hitting Candyman. He parks his car and runs back toward Trashman with gun in hand. He sees Trashman sitting on a pair of steps holding his gun and talking to himself while looking in Candyman's direction. Their eyes meet and Trashman rolls to one side of the steps.

Candyman fires several shots, all missing Trashman. Bullets fly in all directions hitting vehicles moving along in the street. Several vehicles are hit. One of them rides out of control and onto the sidewalk where it crashes into a mail box. Trashman tries to reload his gun. Candyman starts to advance onto Trashman. Trashman sees this and starts running between parked and moving vehicles. Candyman sees that the situation is too dangerous, he stops. In anger, he calls out. "If I don't get you. Somebody else will."

Bertha and Breeze are sitting at the table having dinner. Mark walks into the apartment looking drunk and acting mean. "Where is she?" He blurred out.

Bertha is in shock. "I thought you was still in jail?"

"I know people. They got me out."

Bertha puts on a mean look. "How dare you go to MY job and start a fight with my boss."

"That big mouth had it coming. She talks too much. Besides, that matter was none of your business." He starts walking toward them.

Breeze and Bertha stand. She is holding a knife she was eating with. Breeze steps in front of his mom. "This is what I have been waiting for. I told you if you hurt my mom, you would see the other side of me. Come and see what I have for you."

Mark could barely see Bertha. He pays no attention to breeze. "There you are. You owe me. I'm gonna take care of you first than I'm gonna chew up that little piss ant of yours."

Bertha has one hand on her hip while still holding tight to the knife. "I don't like your attitude and what is it that I owe you? You been eating and sleeping around here for free. I don't want to hear that mess. Leave the key and beat it out of here."

"Yeah," says Breeze. "Get to stepping."

"I ain't leaving and you owe me for everything I've done for you."

Breeze moves up close to stand in front of Mark.

"BREEZE STOP!" She screams. "Before you do something you might regret."

"No mom. I see he didn't get enough of me the last few times. He needs to leave us alone." Breeze turned his back to Mark to look at his mom.

Mark wanted to get at Bertha. He pushed Breeze to one side with force. Breeze falls to the floor groaning. Mark kicks him forcefully. "How do you like that as pay back for what you did to me?"

Bertha can see another fight coming. She screams at Mark. "NO! STOP!" He turns his attention toward her.

Breeze gets up and tackles him to the floor. Bertha watches in horror as Breeze beats Mark about the head and shoulders. Mark is trying to defend himself by trying to block punches Breeze is quickly throwing toward him. Bertha places her hands over her face and walks away. She can hear Mark suffering in the background. Bertha couldn't take it anymore. She comes back into the kitchen and stands near the wall still clutching the knife. The fighting has stopped.

Mark's face is partly bloody. "You see this little bastard? He's gonna grow up to be just like me. Trying to get by in this stupid life." He grabs a bottle from the kitchen table and smashes it. Glass and contents spread out over the floor. He points the broken end at her.

She raised the knife and points it at him. "He'll never be like you! He was right about you all the time. You are a sorry excuse for being a human being."

Mark sees her lowers the knife. He drops the broken end and lunges toward her. With one hand he grip her neck as he pins her up against the wall. His veins pop out of his forehead. He snarls at her. She dropped the knife. Breeze jumps on his back but is knocked to the floor by a side swipe of Mark's hand.

Bertha can hardly breathe. Her voice is very low. "Get-off-me. I'm choking."

Bertha tries to pull Mark's hand off of her. She struggles as he grips her hair with his free hand.

Mark is not willing to let her go. "You thought you could get rid of me that easily, didn't you?"

Breeze watches Bertha from the corner of his eye. He mustered enough strength to get up from the floor with a few shards of glass sticking out of his arm from the fall. He picks up the knife and stabs Mark in the back of his neck. Mark coughs out blood. He releases her from his grip. She slides down the side of the wall. Mark falls to the floor and lays still.

Breeze panics. "Mom!" He helps her up and wells up with tears. He looks down at Mark. "I think he's dead. OH NO!"

Bertha started to shake from a nervous condition. "Baby, are you okay?"

"I'm fine, mom. But he ain't."

An unconscious Mark lay on the floor with blood pooling on the floorboard.

The police arrive alone with the medical services. Bertha talks to the medic as Mark's body, covered in a black bag, is being wheeled out of the building and loaded into a van. Bertha and Breeze go out following the police officer. They walk toward the police car. The police starts to question her. "Tell me what happened?"

"Like I said to the medics, he attack me and my son." Bertha shows the bruises on her neck. The police officer looked at them closely and scratched the back of his head. "It sounds like he had it coming. We been having this kind of problems with him before. We'll write this up as an act of self-defense. However, we're still gonna need you to testify in court."

"I understand." Bertha replied as she held Breeze close to her. They, together, started walking back toward the building.

People standing around outside could be heard talking about gang violence and it was about time somebody had enough guts to start wasting them because the police was letting them have their way around Miller Homes.

Bertha and Breeze walked pass the 'out of order' sign and up the staircase. While walking, Breeze kept looking at his mom. His mine was puzzled. "Why did you tell the police you did it?"

"It's just easier that way. If anything happens, you can't be serving any jail time for that."

"What about you?"

"I'll be fine. I'm not going nowhere if you mean to jail."

"You sure?"

"Yes, I'm sure. I got this under control. So please don't worry."

They walk up the stairs and onto their floor. Breeze looks at their door at the end of the hallway. Breeze paused. "I don't think I can sleep in this home tonight."

"I can understand how you feel. We can go to Auntie's and spend the night. Maybe you'll feel better about this situation tomorrow."

"I hope so."

Buck and Bill was released from jail the next day. Buck walks to Candyman's apartment with a gun in his hand. The door is cracked slightly open. He walks in. "Candyman." He calls out.

Candyman comes out of the kitchen. He stops in his tracks upon seeing buck with a gun. "Woah! What are you doing here?"

"You left us. What kind of boss are you?"

"Buck. Put the gun down."

"I've been doing your dirty work for years. It's time for you to pay up. Them crumbs you been giving me for doing that paper route wasn't worth the troubles I had to go through while you sat back and sucked up all the cream from the top of the money."

Candyman's raises his hands high in the air. Calmly speaking so as not to overly excite Buck. "Take whatever you want."

Buck is still pointing the gun with his finger on the trigger. "You damn right I will. Where's the bag?" Candyman points to the couch. Buck takes his eyes off of Candyman to search for the bag. Candyman takes hold of the gun tucked in the back of his shorts while Buck looks under the couch. He does this with precision so as to not distract Buck.

Candyman pulls the trigger as Buck turned to look at him. Buck falls to the floor unconscious.

CHAPTER Eight

The next morning, birds twittered peacefully from the outside. Bertha and Breeze wake up in a small yellow room decorated with old teenage trinkets surrounding one side of a single size bed. Bertha rises from the bed and walks into the kitchen. Auntie is busy preparing breakfast while humming and old religious tune delightfully.

Bertha see a need to help. "Let me help you with that."

"No. No. I can do it. It's nice having people around here. That room use to be my son's before he died."

Bertha's face dried up. "I'm sorry to hear about that. May I ask what did he die from?"

"Oh. Something happened to him out on the courtyard. I never did get all the details. Anyway, that's alright. It was his time to go. Hopefully, I can join him soon in the new kingdom."

"Oh. You know about the new kingdom?"

She smiled creepily at Bertha. "Girl, I been going to church and reading the Bible. I want to be there when the saints come marching in. Bertha's eyes widen. Breeze walks into the kitchen, hair disheveled. Breeze is scratching his eyes.

Auntie takes notice of him. Sweetly she greets him. "Hey there. Did you sleep well in that room?"

He smiles. "Like a bird in a feather bed." While stretching both arms above his head, he notices the sun light from the curtains is shining on a picture frame of Flash and his Aunt hanging on a wall. His eyes opened wide as he stares at the picture. "How do you know this guy?"

Auntie stopped to look at the picture. "Oh, that's my nephew. He provided for me when my pension wasn't enough. Been taking care of me from the time my son died up until the day he was taken away by the police. Sweetest boy Ever. Why they took him, I'll never know."

Breeze loses interest in the conversion. "Just asking." He is thinking to himself. *'Flash should have been locked up right after birth. He came into this world mean."*

Auntie began setting the table by placing the various breakfast items in the center. Together the three of them sat and enjoyed what was prepared.

Back at the apartment, Bertha has fully decided to take herself and Breeze out of this environment. She calls her doctor to give her the news about leave for good. The Doctor wisher her well and tells her to be sure to check in with a hospital to continue receiving treatments. Also, call her to let her know which hospital she is visiting so her records can be forwarded.

The news reporter returned to Miller Homes following another death. He stood in the courtyard holding a microphone to his face as he looks at a screen picturing Bertha sitting on the witness stand. He gives a summary of what Bertha was saying. "In an attempt to defend herself and her son, Miller Homes' local killers a known drug abuser."

The camera shows a picture of the jury listening to the case.

The reported looks around the Miller Homes area and sees several police officers roaming the area. He speaks into the microphone while showing the area. "Miller Homes is now under constant surveillance."

The mayor climbed out of his car and walked up to the reporter. "The mayor has just arrived. Sir. Would you like to make a comment on this situation?"

The Mayor is given the microphone. "We will not stop until every drug dealer and criminal in this area is put behind bars."

"And there you have it. The words from our mayor." The reporter returned the camera to the screen showing the courtroom. The Judge hits the gavel. Bertha is declared innocent.

Bertha walked out of the courtroom. The news media rush to interview her. She waves her hand toward them giving an indication that she is not willing to make any comments or statements at this time.

Before entering her apartment, Bertha goes to visit Sally for the last time. She knocks on the door. Sally immediately opens it. "What a surprise to see you." She ask her to come inside. " I'm not going to stay long. I was just coming to say I'm taking peoples advice and leaving this town for good."

"OH. I'm so sorry to see you go. I know that that's the best thing for you. Is your son leaving with you?"

"Yeah. He's seems happy. I'm going to miss you as well. I will call you to let you know how my treatments are coming along."

"Please do that."

Well I do have to go."

"I'm so glad you came to tell me you're leaving. I would have been worrying about you if you left without saying anything."

Bertha gives her a hug as she is leaving.

Breeze is sitting on the couch doing his favorite thing. Watching television. Bertha enters. She goes straight to her bedroom, picks up both medications. She hears Breeze has just turned off the set. She rushes out to catch him just as he is opening the front door. "Honey. Will go to the drug store and pick up my medications?"

"Sure mom."

"Wait while I get some money."

"Don't worry mom. I Got this."

"Thanks Son." She heads back toward her bedroom.

He leave by slamming the door close. Bertha jumps at the sound. "Glade to be leaving. That door is driving me batty."

Breeze is walking toward the med store. He smiles to himself and starts thinking. *'Glade to be leaving. No more gangs to think about. And no more craze jobs.'*

Linda and Dee Dee are sitting on Mark's couch continuing to watch the news. The television continued to show news about Bertha's story and Miller Homes. Television flashes external shots of Miller homes and the removal of Mark's body.

The mayor flashes on the screen again. "We will not stop until every drug dealer and criminal is put behind bars."

Linda turned off the television. She whispers a tune. "Free at last. Free at last. I don't know how long this freedom gonna last." Dee Dee breaks out into laugher. Linda starts talking to Dee Dee. "I just knew somebody was gonna do something to him. But not that."

"Girl. Word was out all over town that he was starting trouble. He started slapping on me. I had to put him in his place and he backed off real quick. He knew I don't play that.?"

Linda goes into her room and starts packing her things. Dee Dee walks up to the doorway. I think I'll do the same when I get back to my apartment. Things in this town is falling apart and I don't want to be around when it happens. The next thing that's going to happen is the law will be cracking down on us for working the streets."

"Well. I'm leaving because I ain't got nobody to protect me. And nobody left to pay the rent."

Bertha and Breeze was packing their clothing and other belongings into bags and boxes when Monique came to help.

Breeze was thinking they needed transportation. "Mom. Can I call Candyman to give us a ride?"

"Sure. Use my phone. It's on the kitchen table."

Breeze walked away.

Bertha smiles at Monique. "You didn't have to come and help."

"I know. Really. I didn't know you was packing. I was just dropping by."

"Don't think I was going to leave without saying goodbye to you. We just wanted to get our things together. We only taking our clothes. If you want any of this other stuff, you're welcome to it."

"I'll check it out after you're gone."

Bertha goes to get the apartment key. She gives it to Monique. "Anything you don't want, dump it."

Minutes later, Breeze returned.

Bertha stopped packing and looks up to see what Breeze is going to give for an answer.

"He said no problem. He'll be down by his BMW waiting. Just give him a call when ready. Or if you need help, he can come to help carry some of the stuff down."

"That would be nice of him. But I think we can handle these items."

Monique together with Breeze and Bertha was able to walk out of the building to Candyman's Jaguar with the items. Candyman helped them load the items into the trunk and back seat along with his duffel bag.

Breeze looks at the duffel bag. "You leaving, too?"

"Yeah. This place is going to the dogs. Police are everywhere. Business going down hill. No need to stay and get busted."

Bertha gives Monique a big hug. "I hate to be leaving. I'm going to really miss you and my other friends. But like most people are saying, this is no place to live if you want a better life."

"I know what you mean. Girl, don't worry about me. You know what keeps me going. As long as I can get me a bag of good weed, I'll do fine. Call me some time and let me know how things are going. Don't make it sound too good. I just might come down there and join you, if the weed is better down there then up here." They laugh. Monique became serious. "Please stay on that medication. Let's pray that its working."

"I will. And I might want to keep the weed for myself, if I can't find some really good stuff."

Breeze didn't have much to say except, "Bye Miss Monique."

She gave him a quick hug. "Stay out of trouble and take care of your mom. You hear."

"I will."

Bertha starts to laugh.

Monique looks at Bertha. "What's so funny?"

"You sound so country. 'You hear'. That's just like saying Yall."

"Girl. You know us black folks sometimes use bad language."

Bertha spots Auntie as she is coming down the sidewalk. Bertha tells Breeze and Candyman to wait while she says good-by the Auntie. Auntie is walking along slowly carrying one small bag.

Bertha hugs Monique again and runs off.

Candyman gets Breeze to walk around to the other side of his car away from Monique who starts walking away. He reaches in to his pocket and pulls out a wad of dollar bills. He counts off $1,000 and hands them to Breeze. Breeze is looking amazed. Candyman looks Breeze straight into his eyes. "I should owe you more, but keep that to help your mom out. Don't say anything to her about this until we are out of sight from each other. You got that?"

Breeze is excited. "Thanks Candyman. I don't know how to thank you."

"Don't. We cool."

"Auntie." Bertha calls out. Auntie doesn't hear her. Bertha walks fast to catch up with her. They walk side by side. Auntie look in Bertha's direction. "Oh. How you doing?"

"I'm doing fine. I just wanted to say good-by. Me and Breeze are leaving for good."

"Sweetie. I'm going to miss you and your stories. I hope everything is okay."

"Sure. I'll be okay." Bertha give her a hug and they depart.

Bertha and breeze load themselves into the vehicle. Candyman revved up the engine. An undercover police officer looks at them from across the driveway. Candyman looked back for a second and drive away.

Thee police officer speaks in audibly into his walkie-talkie. He gets into his car. The car follows for one block and turns a corner ignoring the BMW. Candyman looked into his rear-view mirror. Coast clear. He speeds up.

Breeze is in the back seat. He tells Candyman, "You thought they had you for a minute, didn't you?"

They both laugh. "Never my good man."

Bill had made friends with auntie. On occasions, he would stop by to see if she needed any help and also, gets a good free home cooked meal. Bill was having dinner in auntie's apartment when the police knocked once on the door. After no one came to open it, they aggressively knock the door down and rushed in. Bill knew the deal and tried to run out the back bedroom window. Police officers were standing outside by the back window spotted him coming out. He also saw them and crawled back inside. Auntie watched in horror as the police hand cuffed him and dragged him out of the apartment leaving auntie speechless and distraught in her empty apartment.

On Trashman's last days on the streets, he when into the candy store. The girl behind the counter had given him such a hard time that instead of him buying an item, he robbed her of the item and the store's money. What he didn't know was that a hidden camera had ID him and the police was out looking for him. The police patrol roving around Miller Homes had seen him many times walking with some of the tenants and was able to locate him by going to several apartment. A day later, Trashman was finally captured and placed behind bars after assaulting an undercover police officer with a gun on the Miller Homes grounds. While serving his time behind bars, he still continued to be the evil person that he was on the outside. Showing how bad of a person he was tending to be, he spit on another inmate because he didn't like the way the inmate was looking at him. In this type of environment most inmates belong to one group or another. When you do something to one inmate, you are doing it to all of them. The inmate's group looked at Trashman as threateningly. Trashman got so that he didn't like any of them and threw a punch at one of the other inmates. When that inmate started punching back, Trashman ended up getting beaten badly by several other inmates.

Trashman lay on the ground groaning in pain. Eyes swollen and a busted face. Guards came out and placed him in solitary confinement where he will spend most of his prison time.

Breeze and Bertha are seated in the back seat of the BMW with Breeze's head leaning on Bertha's shoulder. Candyman looked at them in his rear-view mirror. He was starting to feel bad that so much had happened to them during their time here at Miller Homes.

They arrive first at the post office where the boxes were dropped off and afterwards went to the train station. Candyman took out the bags from the BMW while smoking on cigarette. The other two climbed from the BMW. Bertha looks at Breeze and then at Candyman.

Bertha walks up to Candyman. "Thank you so much."

"No problem."

Breeze takes his turn and walks up to Candyman. He shakes Candyman's hand. "Thanks for everything."

"You're a good guy. I'm gonna miss you. Be good to your mother. And find a good trade that pays well."

Candyman politely nods at the two while he climbs back into his car and suddenly, the car drives away.

Construction workers were standing outside of Miller Homes. Residents standing behind a fenced in area watched as the buildings were being demolished. A huge wrecking ball hits the front entrance knocking bricks and glass lose that came crashing down to the ground like a storm's wind.

Auntie was standing with some of the residents who have been displaced. "All those memories now history. This is a funny way of protecting us. I never thought they would put me out."

Breeze and Bertha arrive at a quiet little house on the countryside. Bertha's mother, a plump old woman, walked out onto the porch and greeted them with open arms. She gave them a tight hug and helped them inside the house.

Candyman wearing sunglasses along with smoking a cigarette in his mouth was last seen driving down an unknown road. His stash of drugs and money sat in an unzipped duffel bag in the back seat. He looked into the rearview mirror of his BMW toward the city where he had made his small wealth and smiled.

AFTER THOUGHTS ABOUT THE REAL MILLER HOMES

Miller Homes was originally built to house commuters working in and around the Trenton area. However, because of its location, many people felt the location was in a troublesome area where they would not feel safe. So, the city took ownership of the ten story-two development towers and made them available for low income city dweller in need of housing.

The story goes that some of those who moved into Miller Homes had never had a nicer place to call home. They in turn where so use to living in homes that were owned my slum landlords, who took their time in keeping up repairs. The rent was cheap and it was something they could afford.

As time passed over the years, Miller Homes fell into the same category as being one of a number of rundown developments. Performing maintenance in and around the two-high rise became difficult with the rise of gangs making trouble and selling a variety of drugs. Also, the area did not go without a few residents openly selling food and liquor from their apartment to make a little cash on the side. Roughly after some thirty-five years, City Hall had lost control of all activities in the Miller Homes development, and the development has fell into disrepair. Leaving no choice, the two towers were reduced to ruins.

SYNOPSIS

Although Miller Homes II is fictional, it is still a true life story that can presently be seen anywhere in the United States. It continues where the first Book, Miller Homes 'Truth or Fictional' leaves off, which is ninety percent a true story. In the last chapter of the first Book, a young man sits in his BMW watching one of his dealers make a drug deal. That individual in the BMW is a character known as Candyman. A character carried over from the first book. He took over the drug trade around Miller Homes after Sonny Bee and Flash were sentenced to a term each in the State Prison. However, the territory is not easy to claim by Candyman. Trashman, a notorious gangster keeps Candyman on edge as he continues to make trouble in and around Miller Homes.

Bertha had moved to the country side with her children looking for a better life. However, she had been used to being around people and doing things in the community. After spending more than five years in what she called 'No Man's Land,' meaning there were no jobs and very little contact with neighbors, she and her son Breeze returned to East Trenton thinking things would be better.

Bertha goes through many situations that leave her heart and mind headed towards self-destruction. But with the help of her old friend Monique and her new friend Sally, they help her weather her battling situation.

My belief is that what you will retrieve from this story is a sense of what daily problems some people have to endure living in low income government housing. This story can be felt anywhere in the United States, not just in East Trenton.

ABOUT THE AUTHOR

Charles Feggans lived in an area not far from Miller Homes for many years. He would often visit friends there. He knew about the gangs and hustlers. About the police coming many times trying to control bad situations. Miller Homes received its name as "Killer Homes" because the violence that continued to exist until its last days. Charles now lives on the out skirts of Trenton where he helps take care of his grant son part time and has remarried to a wonder lady who supports his efforts.

www.ingramcontent.com/pod-product-compliance
Lightning Source LLC
LaVergne TN
LVHW041942070526
838199LV00051BA/2873